Pride Publishing books by Jon Keys

Leather and Grit
Drawing the Devil
Wrestling with Destiny
Roping in His Heart
Ridden Hard

I0570498

Leather and Grit

RIDDEN HARD

JON KEYS

Ridden Hard
ISBN # 978-1-83943-963-6
©Copyright Jon Keys 2021
Cover Art by Erin Dameron-Hill ©Copyright March 2021
Interior text design by Claire Siemaszkiewicz
Pride Publishing

RIDDEN HARD

Chapter One

Seth sat on the bleachers in the scorching Texas sun, which made him feel like an overcooked piece of beef. But the day's brutal heat was far from his primary concern. What made his legs tremble and shake like an alcoholic at the end of a three-day bender? That would be the frenzy of the rodeo arena located only a few dozen feet away. The clang of metal against metal had become part of the symphony he lived for every summer weekend. Yes, that was the source of the uproar, but the cause was the two-thousand-pound bull trying to break free of its narrow confines.

Anyone who witnessed the scene before him understood. Seth's distilled emotions weren't over the animal itself but the seventeen-year-old cowboy who would shortly be fighting to stay on for eight agonizing seconds.

To put the cherry on the stress sundae, the bull rider who would be trying to keep his seat was...his son.

His friend Travis slid onto the bench beside him. He turned to Seth with a smile. "Zane's having a good run. He drew his bull from one of the best stock operations on the circuit. He should build up some points this round."

Seth studied Travis briefly then shrugged. "I know. We've been doing this since he was big enough to throw his leg over the sheep they ride in the mutton-busting competition. But the lambs have morphed into huge ugly bulls who live to break every bone in Zane's body. It's been the same for years, but somehow, with each rodeo it's more of my focus," Seth said.

"Well, every rodeo puts you nearer to your goal of Zane winning the scholarship he needs to pay for his college education. I can't seem to get my Amy too excited about anything since my divorce from her mother was finalized."

Seth's glance at his friend revealed a troubling change from his typical smart-ass attitude as Travis became lost in his thoughts. The arrangement they had reached years ago when both families had begun competing on the junior rodeo circuit was that they would not be more than supportive friends. He and Travis were in agreement that their kids were the focus, not any potential attraction between the two of them.

With a snort from the bull and the ring of metal against metal, Seth's focus snapped back to Zane as his ride was about to begin.

Zane cocked his head and double-checked his helmet. That was one of Seth's unbendable rules, that he would wear all the safety equipment possible, starting with the helmet and vest. The bull rider's dance began when Zane's head bobbed his readiness and the gate swung open.

The brindle-colored animal with its massive hump paused for a millisecond to identify its targets before exiting the chute with a single jump. Zane stuck his arm in the air like a proud flagpole on Independence Day. The bull filled his part of the contract with leaps and spins Seth would've thought impossible. The animal tang of arena rodeo filled Seth's nostrils. Seth jumped up and down with enough nervous energy to make a hummingbird proud. Then they reached the part of the performance that drove Seth crazy—the other seven seconds of the ride.

He held on to the bleachers with the tenacity of a pack of winter-starved wolves after an elk. The crowd groaned and Seth cringed as Zane swung wide, almost losing his grip. But he knew his son's determination only grew with each competition driving him closer to his goal. Seth ground his teeth together and held his laser-focus through the spectacle. Seth had heard rodeo cowboys called 'modern-day gladiators'. Watching his son, he could see where that came from.

They reached the point where Seth wasn't sure Zane could go any further and the timer went off. It felt like a reprieve from death row.

Seth glanced down just in time to see Zane hit the ground on two feet with his hands thrust above him. That's when he realized Zane had stopped paying attention to the bull. *Bad mistake.* In a split second it had turned and taken aim at his son and was lunging forward with a sound like a diesel engine. Some kind of animal vendetta his son hadn't watched for came to life. Seth wanted to scream, to run into the arena to protect his child, but none of that happened. Zane would have a record-setting shit-fit if he did, and he wouldn't have to anyway. That situation was the exact reason the bullfighter was in the arena. Even better, today's was among the best. Seth was confident everything would turn out fine so long as Shane Neri was in charge. He sprinted toward the bull still wearing some of the clown outfit from his earlier entertainment routine, but this was not a performance. This was life-threatening serious, which was what brought people to the rodeo—to see the rider pitted against the bull and become wrapped in the drama of life and death.

The pickup men charged the bull on their muscular quarter horses, forcing it out of the arena while Shane provided a distraction. It took only seconds. Zane ran for the fence and Shane finished his job.

Travis jumped up and down with excitement while his daughter Amy was relieved that her friend had survived another battle against nature, due in part to Shane's athletic performance.

"It was a fantastic dismount! You can bank on Zane sticking them every time," said Travis while pounding Seth on the back. He dodged the blow from his muscular friend with a laugh. "He's showboating and he knows it. This isn't gymnastics. There are no more points for sticking a dismount. Hell, it's not even called a dismount. It's getting off the bull without being hurt."

"Damn! Did you see that? Shane's an amazing bullfighter," Amy said.

"You got that right, I'm glad he was there when we needed him. I'll help Zane check everything and make sure he can get through his next ride with as few problems as possible," Seth said.

The other two nodded in agreement and the trio made their way off the scorching aluminum bleachers. People underestimated the cumulative impact the unending parade of rodeos had on the contestants.

Most discounted today's performance as just another county fair event in Texas. But the competition's points counted toward the state championship—and a college scholarship.

They left in search of Zane and reached the penning area. It didn't take long before they found him strutting in his leather chaps, swinging his helmet from his hand. He saw Seth and ran to his father, wrapping his arms tight around him.

"Dad, did you see? That bull pulled every trick it had, and I rode right on the edge. It might not have been a perfect ride, but it was a damn good one," Zane said.

"Zane! Watch your mouth. What would your mother think if she heard you talking like that?"

He calmed down, but only a little. "She would tell me it was okay occasionally. Sometimes you even have to drop a big one."

He studied his son and formed a slight smile. "Okay. I'll let you off on that one. She would give you some slack since that was a nasty bull. I'm just glad you're not hurt."

About the time he thought the conversation would end, Travis and Amy chimed in.

"That was amazing. There's no way they won't give you a scholarship. Who else would be better competing for Texas than Zane Davis?" Amy said.

Travis added to the support. "It was a great ride, Zane...one of your best in the last few weeks. Keep it up and you'll win that scholarship."

A smile grew across Seth's face. "You two are getting carried away. Let's get the boy in college and have it paid for with no injuries. That's the basic goal. Once that's accomplished, we can talk about him taking over the ranch and raising his own kids on it." He glanced at Zane, uncertain about what he might see on his son's face at those bits of information.

Travis lifted an eyebrow but resisted any comments about ranch ownership. "Okay, there's only a few more contestants left before they announce the winners of the senior boys bull riding. Let's get a Coke, then we'll see what happens."

None of the next contestants came close to Zane's score, and Travis offered to take everyone out to eat if Zane won. Close by was one of the best taqueria trucks, so devouring tacos might be the activity of the night.

But shortly afterward, it was announced that Zane was the winner for his category, and after the cheering subsided, the teenagers clamored for food, especially the kind that might fill a teenage boy. Travis could remember those days when puberty had left him famished most of the time. They found a favorite truck, not tacos but the best corndogs on the fairgrounds. He'd been waiting in line several minutes when someone called his name. He turned and smiled at a familiar face in the truck waiting to take his order.

"Hey, Cheryl. It's good to see you. How did you end up making corndogs?"

"Oh, you know how it is. The kids are in college and we retired the old man. I thought it would be a perfect chance for me to earn extra Christmas money. Grandma doesn't pay well."

Travis chuckled, "That's ambitious…doing everything this early."

"Yup, that's me. Now, what can I get for you?"

"Well, I have the whole crowd, so hang on."

"No problem, ready when you are."

"We need a corndog for Amy. No, scratch that. Amy wants one hotdog with the neon-green relish." He shook his head. "She loves those things. I don't get it. A corndog each for Seth and me. Then, for the champion junior bull rider four — yes, count them, *four* — corndogs with a side of waffle fries coated in chili."

She finished taking the last of the order and winked at Travis. "Nothing else? A side of beef? Moose?"

Travis chuckled. "Nope. If he wants dessert, I'm sending him back alone."

She laughed then disappeared to fill his request.

Soon he was being passed two paper bags full of food. He spotted his group where he'd left them, under the awning with a picnic table that Seth had located after Zane and Amy had joined them for refueling.

The closer he got, the more uncertain Travis was that he wanted to deal with the hungry denizens he traveled with. They looked like extras from Shark Week. But as soon as they ate, especially Zane, life would be better.

He pulled his food out of the sack, sat beside Amy and doused his meal with a couple of squirts of ketchup and mustard. The meal lasted only a few minutes before the young ones had eaten everything and wanted more. This time Travis was not as congenial.

"It's your turn now. There's plenty of junk food to eat when you get out on the midway. Just watch out for each other, please," Travis said.

Amy gave him a condescending glance and patted his head. "Father, Father… We'll be fine. We are not still the little munchkins from your childhood. Cowboys know how to survive."

"It's not a joke, Amy. People are different now than they were when I was your age. Back in the old days, we had a quarter for a call and people knocked on your door to use your phone because they'd had a wreck. We let them in because it was the decent thing to do. Nowadays I'm not sure you'd get anybody to let you in their house unless you were dripping blood – and probably not even then."

"I was just teasing. Sorry. I shouldn't have done it. I know how that gets your goat," Amy said.

Zane finished the last of the fries, adding ketchup and homemade hot sauce to the chili. He wiped the remnants from his face and turned to the adults. "We recognize what you guys went through. It's not like we don't think about being careful. We'll watch out for each other."

Travis was vacillating – and by the look in Seth's eyes, he was thinking similarly – as to whether their kids were humorous or obnoxious. In the next few moments, Zane and Amy broke into a spontaneous chorus of *We Will Survive*, and the choice for 'obnoxious' was made.

Travis let out a long, exhausted sigh. *Why do I keep trying to educate modern-day kids? Though they don't seem much like kids anymore.* A consolation, if there was one, might be that none of the other parents were in any better situation. Travis' sixteen-year-old girl was wearing him out just as fast as Zane was doing to Seth.

Travis glanced at his watch and waved to their kids. "Go. Have fun. Take care of each other. Yes, I know I've told you the same thing a dozen times. Make your parents happy and pretend to listen – and be back here when we told you to be."

To their surprise, the kids left with hugs and reassurances, even though they sprinted the last fifty feet before disappearing into the midway crowd. Travis watched for a moment, wishing the pair would revert to five-year-olds and come running back to be protected by their fathers. That wasn't happening, Travis knew, but he was sure Seth wished the same thing.

Seth gave him a crooked smile. "We can hope for their safety, and we'll have to keep each other sane in the meantime. I'm feeling too old for the midway, even if it's like Disney on Ice."

Travis smiled and did the two-step for a few feet before motioning Seth ahead of him. "Let's go through the 4-H and FFA exhibits. We can pretend we aren't parents with blood, sweat and tears invested in our children's projects."

"Sounds like a good idea. Maybe it will give us more perspective."

Seth nodded and Travis tried not to react to his endearing expression. It was times like these he wished they hadn't agreed to keep their relationship to just friendship. Travis didn't think he'd mind exploring something more intimate.

Chapter Two

Seth laid out the proposals he planned to add to the presentation brief for the ad agency's client. It wasn't his favorite way to live life, but he did have to work, regardless of the fact that these days he existed for the weekends when Zane competed for rodeo placings. He also found himself being more drawn to Travis, but he and his sixteen-year-old daughter had their own problems. He was certain that managing the family ranch was stressful.

Reflecting on his own career choices left Seth in doubt. Fresh out of college, he had thought he was a good match for the marketing firm, him being as bloodthirsty and cutthroat as any ad man could be. When his wife's cancer had come to dominate their lives, his focus had changed. He'd struggled to cover the expenses. He now believed that his and Zane's choices had become limited once she'd lost her battle.

"Hey, buddy! How are things going?"

Seth cringed and steeled himself to deal with Dave, the person who was his partner on the team for this particular client. "Hey, Dave. How are things this morning? I was just working through the proposal. Is there anything I need a heads-up over?"

Dave's expression hardened as he took the question seriously. "They're an existing account. It should be a slam-dunk. All I have to do was push them in the right direction and they'll be shelling out money to have our brilliant campaign selling their lame product. I mean, who makes a craft root beer in the middle of Texas? What a bunch of damn wimps."

Seth fixed him with an emotionless gaze but Dave went on with the profanity-laced tirade toward their client. Many times Seth had been given no choice but to work with this colleague, whose strategies always seemed to be the strong-arm or the good-old-boy method. Through his monolog, Seth found it easier to ignore the crude man.

When Dave leaned close, Seth got a strong suspicion that he had laced his morning coffee with something stronger than creamer. The sharp aroma of booze filled the air.

"There they are. Those guys are important enough it wouldn't surprise me if Craig dropped to his knees and sucked them off. Our boss is spineless," Dave noted with clear derision.

Seth realized that the conversation was spiraling off in yet another weird and unprofessional direction. At that point he refocused on scanning the client's presentation while Dave continued his rant with a new victim. Seth agreed with him on one point. Craig had never been a good manager. But because Daddy was a Texas oil man and Craig hadn't wanted to go into the oil business, Daddy had located him a business he thought his son could make a living at. Instead, Craig had spent years destroying the successful firm his father had bought. Bloodthirsty wasn't always the best business model, even in advertising. But now Craig was getting closer to retirement and the firm seemed to be struggling more in the new Texas economy.

"Okay, Seth. Let's go bust some balls and sell root beer."

A cold chill washed over him when he realized Dave was back to paying attention. "So, what's the plan today, Dave.? You'll be pitching for the whole team? I know you don't like the client, but I think Craig wants them."

Dave motioned toward him. "It's all there and just needs some polish, but I nailed it all down for you."

The shock washed over Seth as he studied the proposals he'd been working on all day, thinking he had the final version, only to find that Dave had changed his work. He remained speechless when Craig appeared. "All right, boys. Let's reel this one in."

* * * *

Two hours later the results of their meeting stupefied Seth. In that short time, the clients had fired them then marched out of the door. Now he waited to see how bad the fallout would be from losing the account.

Seth struggled with the idea that he was about to lose his job. If that happened, he wasn't sure what he and Zane would do. He would have lost his safety net. Anna's treatments had wiped out any savings they'd had. They were living paycheck to paycheck. Now, with this disaster, he didn't know how they'd survive.

He wasn't even clear if he and Zane could keep their house.

Seth knew this could be the end of his career at 'Assholes-r-Us'. The entire account team was waiting in dread to see who would be axed.

A group of vice presidents was meeting to review the disaster and assign blame. The day crept along as Seth tried to keep busy and unobtrusive. But his reprieve ended when Craig appeared at his cubical. He was certain this wouldn't be something he'd be happy about.

"They informed me we lost the Hill Country Root Beer account—what should've been an easy spiral for a homerun." He stared at Seth for a long minute before he continued. "You've been with me for years, Seth, and handled some of my bigger clients. Firing you with the rest of the team, even though one of the team members was more than happy to toss you under the bus, didn't seem prudent. But I decided it's your job to do whatever it takes to get the root beer company back on board as a client. Do I have your guarantee you'll accomplish that task?" Craig asked.

Craig's expression wasn't one Seth had seen often over his years at the firm. There was little latitude on this assignment, to be sure.

"Get your team organized. The idea of unemployment should inspire you, so choose your new group with care. Get busy. I want George and his son back in the fold and thinking we're the best ad agency in North Texas sooner, not later."

Seth pursed his lips into a tight line. He met Craig's stare then cast a glance over the entire room. Without another word, Craig returned to his glass-walled corner office overlooking the Dallas skyline. Seth composed himself briefly then began creating the team to bring Hill Country Root Beer back to them as a client.

He set to work.

It didn't take long for Seth to reach his limit and he left the office, taking the file. As he closed the door to his car, a tear formed in the corner of his eye and rolled down his cheek.

I don't know how much longer I can keep this up. But at least I avoided the head man's ax today.

The drive home seemed longer than usual, and Seth had the disastrous meetings playing on a loop in his mind.

He was emotionally spent by the time he walked into his living room, tossed the day's mail on the table then flopped into his recliner with a whoosh of air. He looked at the folder that held the details of the disastrous meeting. *How could I lose the best client I had for the firm?* At least Seth thought he might have a chance with George, the father of the Hill Country Root Beer pair. He believed that the older man might be more likely to overlook the blunder than his son. Seth hoped they'd be open to giving him another chance and wouldn't immediately choose a different agency to represent them.

When Zane had been younger and had lost his mother, Seth had promised both of them he'd do whatever it took to make Zane happy. This 'save the client' situation fell directly into that category. He couldn't lose his job. It was times like these that he was glad Zane's mother was not around to see what a disaster he had created. He stood looking out of the window toward the typical suburban neighborhood that had been their home for the last eighteen years.

Today he might have erased the future he had planned for their life in the house.

He sat in the chair for several minutes before deciding that if he didn't get up then, he would still be sitting in the chair when Zane got home from his after-school activities at the high school. He dug the critical folder from the leather briefcase he loved. It had been a final gift from his wife. He started through the information he had gathered when the account had been passed to him. Root beer wasn't a passion for Seth, but this company should have been an easy client. As he went further, Seth realized he hadn't made any serious blunders. As he went through each page, his anger grew. It became more and more obvious that Dave had screwed up his handling of the account.

After about an hour of unproductive work, Seth decided he needed to get out of the house before he made choices he would regret. Zane would be back before too long and he didn't want to make his son's stress worse. Besides, Zane would try to help him, and advice from a seventeen-year-old boy was highly questionable. He was a good boy, though, and Seth appreciated him.

He slammed the paperwork he was studying against the top of the heavy wooden desk. He was getting nothing done and needed a distraction. Seth glanced around the room, trying to find something that might give him the kind of change he needed, and it occurred to him that he hadn't been running in quite some time. A brisk circuit of a mile or two would be good to take his mind off anything.

He had enjoyed the sport of cross-country when he'd been in high school, even though he was built bigger than the typical cross-country athlete. The fact that he was on the wrestling team made the difference obvious. He walked over to his dresser and started looking through the clothes inside. After a few minutes he found what he was looking for, and to his surprise, his running gear was still in good shape. He gathered everything he needed, tossed it onto the bed and started stripping. He chucked his work clothes into the laundry basket. A few minutes later he was down to the athletic supporter he wore as part of his regular undergarments.

Seth looked at the almost-fluorescent jockstrap he'd chosen and had to smirk. It looked like something a ten-year-old boy would wear to show off his barely developed goods. But regardless, it wasn't long before he was ready to begin his run. It didn't disappoint him that his combination of athletic wear did an outstanding job of showing off his well-developed equipment.

There was a running path of easily more than a mile that ran around the common grounds of the housing complex. Seth had every intention of completing it more than once as he trotted to the beginning of the path. He followed the small trail that took him to the trailhead where stretching equipment had been installed. Once he was ready, Seth started off at a slow pace, thinking about his day as he reviewed the various events. It didn't take too long. Though, before he let the day's events go and he was lost in the run. By the time he reached the halfway mark, Seth was feeling the effects of the off-time he'd taken from his former everyday activity. If he had let the intervals between practice sessions accumulate any longer, he'd be performing like a rank beginner. Sweat was making rivulets as it ran across his bare torso while he made his way over the gravel path.

By the time he was at the three-quarter-mile mark, the top of his running shorts was drenched with sweat. He ran his fingers through his hair, enjoying its casual feel that was much different from the way it was styled for the office. By the time he reached the next hill, Seth wasn't sure he should be running through the scorching Texas landscape much longer. The sensations he was feeling had gone from invigorating to painful. Seth made it to the end of the first lap and decided that it was all his body could deal with for the day. He stood, gasping for air, as he worked to catch his breath for a few minutes. Once he stopped heaving, he began to walk through a cool-down.

Seth found himself with company — a pair of college runners whose parents lived in the neighborhood. Seth recalled that they had left for a local community college and had disappeared from the group of local runners. They seemed as surprised as he was for them to encounter each other on the trails. Their horseplay made Seth wonder what they were actually after, because their running trunks were thin and nearly transparent. Brian's was particularly revealing, consisting of two straps framing his ass and a pouch holding his goods.

"Hey, Josh, Brian. How are you doing? It's too hot to be racking up many miles today."

They looked up from their play and shot Seth a grin. "Just for a quick one. It's too fucking hot for a good pounding."

Seth stood for a few seconds longer. The men reminded him of some of Travis' traits that he found so attractive. Travis' ability to behave like an adult didn't hurt either. Also, Seth wasn't into the tiny physiques that the long-distance runners sported. He realized the conversation was making him miss Travis and he cut the conversation short. It was obvious they were looking for a place to make out. "Well, have a good run. I need to clean up and go see a friend of mine."

With a final wave of his hand, Seth started toward his home at a trot.

Going to see Travis was always fun for him. He'd always found the cowboy lifestyle fascinating. That might be why he hadn't minded Zane pursuing the bull-riding dream. Even though it was outside his comfort zone, he liked to dress the part of the cowboy — or at least his interpretation of how a cowboy should dress.

Their friendship had started when their children had both joined the junior rodeo association, and he and Travis had built a good-enough friendship that they'd shared their deep dark secrets regarding their sexual orientation, that they were both bisexual. At the same time, they'd decided it would be in everyone's best interest if they made the decision to remain just friends. Even though they had agreed to keep it at that back then, today Seth had begun really wanting it to be a lot more.

After he'd gotten home, he had a quick shower and looked through his closet for the right outfit for what he planned. Seth studied the rack of custom-made cowboy boots he'd accumulated over the years. In traveling across Texas, Seth had picked up some western wear he was pleased to own. He stood in front of the full-length mirror, looking first one way then another. After a few minutes, he decided he was satisfied with the look and headed out of the door. It wouldn't take long to drive to Travis' ranch, and his friend had a knack for bringing out the humor in any situation. Seth needed something to smile about.

Once Seth arrived, he had no trouble finding Travis. Plumes of cuss words and cries of pain left no doubt as to where his friend was and what he was doing. Travis was good at many things but machinery repair was not one of them. Once Seth located him, he stood listening to one of the more inventive collections of vintage profanity, then the shop went silent.

"Who's out there? Don't try and hide. I'll find you quick enough."

He stepped around the corner to find Travis entwined in the guts of a vintage John Deere baler. Seth couldn't help but admire his bronze torso, even if at this time it was liberally smeared with what had probably been the original lubricant used on the equipment. Seth gave himself a few seconds to enjoy the sight sprawled before him. Travis had stripped off his shirt at some point, and Seth took advantage of the opportunity to admire the view.

Travis' fit body left him again questioning their agreement from the past. He licked his lips as he took in Travis' chest with its perfect fan of hair, merging into a darker treasure trail that plunged into his jeans with a bulge that presented him with yet another part of Travis to lust over. But it was time for him to act like a grown-up and quit drooling like a teenager.

Seth cleared his throat and Travis looked up at him with an expression marked with chagrin. "Well, I guess you caught me using some pretty bad language this time. Working on the machinery shouldn't be a big deal, and it's sure not my favorite thing. But if I don't get it to work, I won't be able to harvest what little hay we have, and the winter reserves will be even less."

Seth considered the situation for a minute and decided he needed to focus on Travis' needs. In the short time since he'd arrived, he could tell the situation on the farm was becoming a major problem for Travis. "What can I do to help you? There was a point in my life that I could work on a car. It was the only way I had something to drive when I was in high school."

Travis stared at him for a few seconds before snickering. "It's funny to think of you buried headfirst trying to fix a muscle car."

"Well, believe it or not, that's what happened. But I haven't had a wrench in my hand since I left for college, so I don't know how much help I might be."

Travis studied him then shook his head. "Doesn't matter what you did before. It would be great to get some help. Not with the clothes you're wearing right now, though. This old baler will screw them up in no time. They're practically church clothes."

Seth snorted. "I don't think you know our church, but I'm happy to help you."

Travis glanced at him again. "If you insist. But there's no way I'm letting you work on that old piece of equipment in a pair of custom-made boots. I think we're about the same size. Take a look in the walk-in closet in my bedroom and see if you can find a pair of work boots. An old pair of Ropers would be fine."

Seth made his way to Travis' room. The smell of leather filled his senses, distracting him pleasantly for a moment. Remembering his goal, he found a pair of boots and slipped them on. Once he'd pulled on the comfortable footwear, he took a moment to glance around the bedroom. It wasn't like he hadn't been there before. There was no doubt in his mind that Travis had decorated the room, not his ex-wife. Travis had more than his share of Frederic Remington and Charles Russell art to keep him mindful of his family's place in Texas history. He made his way back to where Travis was working and stood quietly, becoming more and more confident that he could help. After about the third time Travis took the skin off one or two of his knuckles, he stepped up and took the ratchet from the cowboy.

"Let me give it a try before you don't have any skin left on your knuckles."

Travis waiting for only a brief time before he handed the tool over with a sigh. "Dad was amazing at keeping everything running. I don't have his gift, and I don't see Amy gathering around trying to learn how to hotwire a pick-up anytime soon either. You couldn't possibly do any worse than I am, and I thought it was going to be something simple, like maybe a gear or a tine broke."

Seth motioned for Travis to step back and let him look. He was very happy to discover that the baler was simpler than a car engine…much simpler. It really was just a series of belts and gears that kept everything running. After studying it for about ten or fifteen minutes, he thought he could fix the issue. "I think this is actually pretty simple, at least within the scope of my high school auto-shop days. But I don't know your setup here, so you may have to play fetch and carry."

Travis stared for several long seconds before he blurted out, "You can fix it? Without bringing in some high-dollar repair guy from John Deere? That would be amazing. Just let me know what you need, and I'll find it. The shop's pretty complete. It was just the mechanic who wasn't doing too well."

Seth gave Travis a huge grin. "Well, let's start with something easy then. How about a complete ratchet set?"

"That one I know, boss." Travis took off at a run to the shop building and was back in almost no time. He returned with a long green box and held it out toward Seth, opened the snaps then lifted the lid to reveal the rows of shining chrome cylinders that filled the space. Seth inspected them briefly then shot Travis a smile. "Perfect! Now let's see what we can do about getting you back into the fields before there's no hay left."

With Seth and Travis working together, the job progressed rapidly, although Seth was quickly reminded that he hadn't worked with anything of this kind for at least twenty years. What would have been an easy chore when he was in high school was more difficult on an unknown type of machinery, even if it was a little more simplified. He also found those sharp shards of metal Travis had been locating all morning had been placed there by the devil, just to aggravate hard-working men.

It was close to noon by the time they'd repaired the baler, and there was just a single nut to place to finish the work.

He put the nut and socket together, then turn to Travis. "You're ready to finish this thing off?"

"Damn right I am."

Seth handed him the tool then watched as Travis threaded the last nut into the piece of equipment. He stood, stretched his back and let out a low groan. He looked at Seth with a satisfied grin. "I'm getting too old for this stuff. I can't work on equipment without wearing myself out. A couple of hours under a piece of machinery and I can't stand up straight."

Seth couldn't help but let his eyes flicker over Travis' torso before returning a thoughtful gaze. "I have another skill you don't know about, but I think you would appreciate it."

Travis picked his shirt up from where he'd dropped it earlier and smiled at Seth. "Oh? What might this magical talent of yours be?"

"I give the best back rubs in northern Texas," Seth said.

Travis stretched again, lifting an eyebrow as he studied Seth. "That good?"

"Well, at least I won't make it worse."

"If you're offering, I'll take you up on that," Travis replied.

He motioned Seth ahead of him, kicking off his boots at the door and tossing the well-worn T-shirt into the laundry before heading to the master bedroom. By the time Seth followed, Travis was in the midst of stripping off his underwear and dropping them to the floor.

Seth gave himself a few seconds to appreciate the man's physique. His tight butt with just a bit of hair was definitely appealing, but Seth didn't want to get caught peeking after all the promises they'd made to each other. He cleared his throat as Travis kicked away the last bit of clothing.

"Where are the towels?" Seth asked. "Some baby oil maybe? I doubt you have any massage oil."

Travis tugged at his low-hanging ball sac and motioned toward a chest of drawers. "You might take a look there. I doubt there's any massage oil, but there might be some baby oil."

Seth motioned Travis toward the bathroom as he made his way to the dresser. "Go clean up. A good hot shower will loosen you up and make my job easier."

Not that you can do anything with that body to keep me from being interested.

Seth set the baby oil he'd found on the nightstand. He'd already laid a towel over the bed and another in the bathroom for Travis. Someone entered the room and he turned to see Travis, fresh out of the shower and drying himself from head to toe. He was running the towel over his crotch when he looked up and saw Seth standing in front of him.

"Well, you were right about the shower. I feel better now." Travis tossed the towel back into the bathroom, looked at Seth and asked, "Where do you want me next? I'm ready for whatever you have in mind."

Seth shook his head, surprised at the wording he'd used. *I could only hope that you're ready for what I'd have in mind, given the chance.* But the look Travis was giving him was one that didn't seem to hold any double meaning. "Get on the bed, face-down. I don't have one of those fancy massage beds where you can stick your face in the hole, but I'm sure we can figure out something."

Travis climbed on the bed without further instruction and lay across the towels with his head nestled in his crossed arms. Seth lifted the bottle of baby oil, popped the cap on the top and began squirting it over Travis' back.

"Shit, it's cold."

Seth chuckled. "Give it a second. The oil will warm up. Besides it's a pretty warm day. I'd think the cool oil would feel good."

The grunt he got in return didn't give Seth a clear answer, but it didn't matter anyway.

He started working the oil from Travis' waist to the hairline on the back of his neck. At first Seth sensed a little hesitancy, then Travis apparently warmed to the work he was doing and let out a low moan.

"Damn, that feels good. If you do that for an hour or so…" Travis said with another groan.

"I was hoping you'd enjoy it. I never want to leave my client wanting more."

Seth worked his palms into the tight musculature of Travis' back and shoulders. The oil soaked his skin until Travis' upper torso was coated. He decided it was time to try something more…interesting.

He took one of Travis' ass cheeks with his hands and started rubbing it with some intensity. It didn't take long before Travis filled the room with long moans. Seth kept working on him, beginning with his feet and sliding higher up his legs until the only thing that wasn't oiled like a diesel was between Travis' legs.

That was when he realized that the work he'd been doing was having its effect on more than just Travis. Seth had managed to work himself up quite a head of steam, and his cock was jutting out like a new cane pole. It was time to back out of this situation without embarrassing either one of them.

Unfortunately, he wasn't sure how to manage that goal. If they went any further, he was likely going to pop if he didn't get himself under control pretty soon.

Seth picked up the towel beside the bed and tossed it over Travis like a warm wool blanket. Travis squirmed underneath the covering before he turned back to Seth. His face was flushed, and his breathing was intense. Travis stumbled on his words for a few seconds before saying, "Great job, Seth. I think I can walk around for the rest of the day now."

Travis stood and tucked the towel tight around his waist after using one of the corners to dry his ears. "It occurred to me you probably didn't start out here to help me fix that old baler. Was there something you needed to see me about?" Travis asked.

Seth tried to avoid the truth of his originally intended conversation. He wasn't sure he wanted to share his crappy work situation with his friend. Seth turn to Travis, shaking his head. "It really wasn't that big a deal, honestly. I was going out to whine about my bad day. It's likely that you've had one that's worse."

Travis studied Seth for several minutes as he continued to dry off with a fresh towel. Seth found himself becoming more interested in what was being revealed as the covering slipped lower than by anything else. Seth was ready to dismiss the entire idea when Travis dropped the towel and stood naked in front of him.

"Come on, Seth. We been at this for a long time. You know you can trust me, and I might be able to help you."

Seth let out a growl of frustration. "Well, first thing, I can't talk to you while you're standing there in your birthday suit. I know we've had a hands-off policy since the kids were little. But they're not little anymore and…"

Travis stared at him for a few seconds before he stammered out, "Are you s-saying you might be interested in something a little m-more adult?"

"Yes! You just name the time and location. Hell, we could go at it right now and I could show you a few tricks." But before the conversation could go any further or Seth decided to try to use the rod stretching across the front of his pants, he said, "But I think we've had enough revelations for now. For now, let's leave things as they are and harvest what hay we can for you."

"Oh no you don't,. You came here for a reason. I'm not gonna let you escape without telling me what's going on. I can tell something is bothering you. We've been hanging around each other longer than just about anyone else, and you're the best friend I have. We'll deal with the new revelation another time. But for now, spill it. What's happening?"

Seth tried to think of a way to distract Travis, but after spending years around the cowboy, he was certain his friend wasn't going to be distracted. Seth sighed. "We lost one of our best clients and I was team leader for the project. Craig told me I have one chance to fix it or I can pack up my desk and not worry about coming back."

Seth tried to pull himself together before finally he gave up. There was no way he was going to have any more of the conversation with Travis standing in front of him looking hot as hell — and still naked. "Look... I'm more than willing to have this conversation with you, but you've got an unfair advantage. You have to put on at least a few clothes...please." Seth's gaze drifted down Travis' torso again. He closed his eyes and waved toward the closet. "Put on something. This just isn't okay." He'd been the one to blurt out about taking their relationship in a sexual direction but he wasn't ready for that discussion today. He motioned Travis toward the closet again. "Go. Before both of us do something we might regret."

"What makes you think I'd regret it?" Travis asked.

Seth's face turned red at Travis' innuendo. *This really might happen some day!* But right now it was time to nip the whole situation in the bud. "All right. Get dressed.

We still have things to do." He had to get the subject changed, at least for today. "Hey, what are we doing next, anyway?"

"Like you mentioned, there's a little bit of prairie hay we can bale. It isn't much, but it's better than nothing." Travis finished dressing in clean clothes and made his way toward the door. He paused there and turned to Seth. "You ever put up hay?"

"No, I pretty much grew up a city kid."

Travis smiled. "Have you ever tried pulling a rake behind a half-century-old tractor?" Without giving Seth an opportunity to reply, Travis disappeared out of the doorway with his laughter echoing back to the room.

Chapter Three

Seth sat on the top rail of the arena fencing with Travis leaning close beside him, seeing the competition from a different angle. This was their third rodeo in as many weeks and they were there to support the Junior Rodeo Club. The group was comprised of local kids, including their own, who appreciated any help they could get. The bronc rider who was queuing up was Daniel Donovan, who had as much experience as Zane and Amy. Daniel was a year or two younger than Zane, and even though he rode horses instead of bulls, he'd always helped push Zane by passing along any suggestion he felt would be helpful, and everyone in the club would do the same for each other. They were a competitive bunch but wanted everyone to perform well.

Seth watched in silence as Daniel finished his ride prep, getting the last of his gear in place. He had help from some other contestants, so Seth allowed his attention to drift.

He shifted his gaze from the young cowboy to a man sitting by himself in the bleachers. He nudged Travis then nodded toward the obviously stressed parent. "Kirk still doesn't handle the pressure of Daniel in competition very well, does he?"

"He may be a tense parent, but he's hot," Travis replied.

"I can agree with that assessment for days," Seth said.

Travis smacked Seth with the back of his hand. "Stop it! All you're going to do is stir up trouble if you don't quit that. I'm not sure how well it would go over if half the parents were sleeping with each other."

Seth bumped Travis. "Lord, the number of them I'd hook up with is real short."

Travis let out an unrepentant chuckle. "I've resisted my male urges so far, but there's only so long you can keep a good piece of ass away from a determined country boy."

Seth smirked. "It's hard to keep a determine city boy away from that butt too. It's not like everything is dead from the waist down, but I don't want to cause any straight-boy trouble." Seth paused for a second, then continued. "But back in my college day, I would've tapped that ass before lunch during freshman orientation."

The comfortable way Travis handled his fantasy interaction with the other parent left Seth with an ache he hadn't realized was growing, even though he'd played along with the conversation. His attention was pulled back to the competition when, at one point, the horse almost climbed out of the chute. Its body arched until it was U-shaped. Seth glanced over to see how Kirk was handling the spectacle involving his child and found him nearly curled into a fetal position.

The ride was one of those eight-second ones that seemed to go on for an eternity. Kirk's son Daniel was one of the up-and-comers in the rodeo club. Seth wanted to do all he could to encourage him and his dad. The vignette played out to its conclusion. At the end of his ride, Seth would have rated it...adequate. Then he had to remind himself that part of Zane's competition style was showboating, and he really couldn't compare the two.

The crowd broke into a cheer when Daniel landed then waved his hat in the air. One thing about being a bronc rider was that the horse might run over you in its excitement, but a rank bull would intentionally hunt down a cowboy.

"How did he do?" asked Kirk, who'd risen to join them. "The first round went pretty well, I thought. The second one wasn't as impressive. But what did *you* think? He's still working out some details, isn't he?"

Travis gripped the anxious father by the shoulders, fighting to keep from laughing. "Kirk! Calm down. Daniel did great. He should be in the money today."

"Is that possible? Coming close is exciting. Just breaking into the top ten would give him such a boost to his ego."

It wouldn't hurt Seth's day if Zane had some success too, but he didn't say that out loud. "You've got a good chance...really a better-than-average chance. Hang in there. There are only a few more riders."

Travis nodded in agreement. "Daniel did great. He's starting to hit his stride. You guys will see a lot more wins than losses from here on out. That would be my assessment."

Kirk responded like a five-year-old with the new all-day sucker. Seth laughed when he started dancing in the middle of the aisle from sheer excitement. But Seth couldn't help but notice the bubble butt that showed on the backside of his athletic body. Beyond that, he kept any more speculation to himself. Seth had never considered his gaydar to be worth a crap, so he wouldn't make a prediction. And besides, the man wasn't Travis. Then he realized Kirk had disappeared, probably running to see what he could do for his son.

Seth glanced at Travis and shook his head. "That man is exhausting. He's wound tighter than a New Mexico rattler."

"He isn't helping Daniel either. But I'd still nail that ass," Travis said.

Yeah, but I'd rather you nail mine.

The Junior rodeo twisted its way toward conclusion with a win for both Amy and Zane. Seth and Travis glowed with excitement at being among the winners, but for Zane and Amy, part of the fun was the rides and food trucks. The whole club wanted to go, but Seth refused to be responsible for ten or twelve kids whose parents wanted a free babysitter. He and Travis had decided that they'd only be responsible for their own offspring.

Amy had been on the midway the past three nights. She had her list of favorite rides she wanted to hit during the final night. Travis gave their kids the rules, which were simple. "No more than two hours and only the two of you. You can take my truck, and you're back at the room before midnight."

Seth nodded. "That's right. Don't pimp out the truck for rides or you'll be grounded for the next six months with nothing but school and rodeo practice."

Before Seth could add any additional conditions, their kids escaped the motel room and were peeling out as they left the parking lot in Travis' pickup.

"How new is that truck?" asked Seth.

"New. Really new."

"I was afraid so."

* * * *

"Dad, we need to get started. Amy didn't get any practice runs yesterday because we ran out of time. I was thinking she would go first today."

Seth nodded, bringing his focus back to the arena at Travis' ranch. "That's a good plan. We don't want to impose on Travis and Amy's goodwill. I can see the improvement since you've had bulls to practice on between rodeos."

"No, there is no doubt of that. They're helping me out so much. I hope they know some of my winning is because of their help."

There was a familiar voice behind them. They turned to see Travis had joined them. "I wouldn't go that far. You ride in an arena we already have and didn't use. It's not that big of a deal."

Seth waved away Travis' explanation. "We appreciate the assistance, but I don't want to become one of *those* people. We already owe you for keeping back the bulls for Zane's practice."

Travis caught his breath then released it slowly. "Everything worked out fine. You two need to stop worrying so much about us. Maybe it's just me, but Amy doesn't have the fire in her belly for rodeo like Zane does. That's okay. Not everyone is meant to do that kind of competition."

Seth was always embarrassed when he tried to talk about anything regarding help with Travis. But he decided that was silly, because he and Zane had been there to help Amy out through her whole development. It seemed to be the best way to keep a strong friendship.

"It's hot and today's forecast is for high humidity. The heat index yesterday was around a hundred and ten. Let's get this all started before today's temperature kicks our butt."

Seth nodded in agreement and motioned them toward the arena. Travis had already set up for Zane's runs. He had the three bulls they'd kept for Zane's practice lined up in the chute. They lined the fence while Zane put on his gear down to the chaps and secured his helmet. Everyone knew Seth wouldn't tolerate any kind of sloppy safety protocols just because none of these bulls were as vicious as the ones that contractors brought to the events. As soon everything was in place, he climbed the fence, and Travis stood outside the chute, ready to open the gate when Zane signaled. Seth watched him go through a checklist then settle onto the animal's back. He signaled to Travis with a nod of his head.

The animal jumped onto his front feet, his rear hooves slicing through the air, showing an impressive first maneuver that Zane had to deal with. What the animal was doing was more exciting than anything they had expected today. Seth smiled when Amy let out a low whistle and said under her breath. "Damn. That boy can ride."

The yellow bull pushed Zane to his limits. His son would have gained an impressive number of points on this ride if it would have happened in competition. Amy held the stopwatch as the final couple of seconds ticked off. The bull was in the middle of yet another jump when Amy cried out "*Ding ding ding ding.* That's it. Hit the ground. Zane one, bull nothing."

Zane considered the bull's movements for a few more seconds, waiting for an opportunity to dismount. His son leaned forward and let the bull's jump give him the momentum he'd been waiting for. Zane landed, in control. He paused for a second, hat in hand for the effect.

Zane glanced over to see Amy shaking her head and his father and Travis giving him a thumbs-up.

The second ride went fairly smooth, and Seth's pride for his son swelled.

It wasn't long before Zane slipped over the railing and onto the third and final bull.

While he waited for Zane's last ride, Seth remembered the conversation he'd had with Travis about helping. He hoped the growing relationship between him and Amy would give him an opportunity to do what he could to balance the scale.

"Hey, Amy, is everything okay? Anything I can do?"

"No, nothing you can help with." For a second Amy seemed lost, gazing into the distance, then she turned Seth. "Puberty. Girl stuff you don't want to deal with."

Seth gave her shoulder an affectionate squeeze. "If there's ever something I can do, you let me know. I'm always here for you. Promise me?"

She nodded then motioned toward the final bull, which was fastened into the chute. "They're ready."

Seth turned his gaze to the small bull Amy had directed him toward. He wasn't sure where Travis had found this new one. His entire herd was Angus, and this bull was a Hereford. Regardless, it didn't take long before they had the bull ready. Seth had made himself a few notes on Zane's first and second rides, but this time, he focused even tighter on the performance. Seth turned to Amy with a questioning expression apparently clear on his face.

Amy glanced at Seth and let out a giggle. "This is a new bull. Dad bought it at the local auction. It was staring at the seller's fences and trying to get to the heifers. He's also more contrary than the other two. Zane will find him more challenging than the yearlings from our herd."

The ring of the metal bell was louder than the others, even though the dance was similar. The bull arched his neck and settled into a series of jumping spins that left Zane moving like a bobblehead toy. It might be more of a challenge than Zane needed. Seth wasn't sure where the bullfighter would come from to save Zane.

It horrified him to see Zane hanging on with both hands, clinging to the bull's side.

Seth waited as long as he could. It was time to go into full-on dad mode and save his son — or go down trying to save him, at least. He vaulted the fence and took out at a dead run for the mix of man and bull. He was getting close when, in the blink of an eye, the bull changed his strategy and attacked him.

I'm targeted. Oh shit. Shit.

Seth told himself that it was nothing more than an adult round of dodgeball — one he would win. He waved his hands to make certain he kept the bull's attention. With a little luck, the tactic would give Zane a few seconds to get himself back onto the arena floor. He glanced back and found that Zane was still on the animal.

"Get off! The ride's over," he yelled at Zane. Then it hit Seth.

Zane had gotten himself tangled in the rigging trying to get free from what was becoming a terrible situation. The bull kept his eyes and attention focused on Seth, who wasn't sure how, but he would rescue his son. They'd already had enough pain and sorrow for a lifetime. He wasn't losing his boy.

Travis came from the side at a dead run. While Seth focused on rescuing Zane, he realized that for once he had support from someone else.

"Keep him distracted, Seth. I'll get Zane loose in just a second."

With a sharp tug, Travis got Zane's hand off the rigging. By the time Travis caught Zane, the fall had knocked the breath out of him. But after Seth ran the bull safely out of the arena, he rushed over to kneel beside him.

"You okay? That was close. You could have been hurt, or…"

Travis took the hand Seth offered and lifted himself to his feet. Seth stared at him in gratitude. "You saved Zane."

"Nothing you wouldn't have done. Let's just make sure he's okay."

* * * *

Travis sat at his desk with layers of paperwork spread out before him, but he was prepared. From what he could tell, what he'd gathered should cover everything needed for a loan request. The year had been another in a string filled with drought. The bank had to see the necessity of helping ranches like his through the scorching summer.

He vaguely heard someone enter the room, but he was so focused that he didn't register beyond anything that. The new arrival grasped the back of his neck and started massaging. He resisted for a few seconds then he dropped his head forward and let out a low sigh.

"Whatever you're doing, keep doing it. We could bottle it and sell it on Harry Hines Blvd. in Dallas. That might be one way to recover from the worst of the cattle market for the last several years."

"Well, Dad, I guess we could sell it. Most courts in Texas would consider it prostitution, though." Amy giggled.

"Then there's my daughter, who is too smart for her own good. What am I going to do with the little girl who was afraid of pigs because she believed they would make her into sausage?"

"Dad! I was only two, and Piggly Wiggly scared me, a lot. This conversation is getting weird though. What can I do to help?" Amy said.

Travis refocused on the piles of paperwork organized across the desk and spread over the floor with the landmines of items he was trying to organize. He needed to explain choices he'd made and had to condensed what he'd been doing with his life into a two-page document. But all he could do was stare at Amy and shrug.

"I don't know what the bank will say today, but I have everything together that Frank asked for, plus some extra." He turned toward Amy and lifted one eyebrow. "Including the fact that my daughter is a state rodeo champion in barrel racing and pole bending. There are a lot of things in Plan B that would justify a short-term loan to get us through this summer."

He stared at her for a few seconds before breaking into a grin and continuing. "The spring calves will be ready to sell in a few months. There you go. Cash on its way."

"Okay, okay. I give up," Amy said. "I'll leave you to suffer in quiet. Let me know if I can do anything else."

He motioned her toward the door. "Go have a good day. Don't worry about your dad. I'll get this all worked out. I don't need my sixteen-year-old daughter to have the same stomach issues her father has."

An answer by email would help with the nerves but something in him wanted his answer face to face. He would like to think he could save the ranch. He glanced around the room, considering how things had changed since he'd tagged along with his grandfather—when the banker had been *his* ally.

But that wouldn't work now. He'd been ready to talk to the banker two weeks before but had been sent home with a stack of paperwork to finish. He realized the person he considered his banker was nothing more than a glorified teller. They would go through the paperwork, Travis felt sure of that. But the days of asking for a fifty-thousand-dollar loan and securing it with the shake of the hand was long gone. He glanced around, realizing he needed to get this trip under way, so he headed into town, and in less than an hour later, he found himself sitting in the pickup and dreading the impending conference. He left the truck and made his way into the bank.

"Hey, Travis. How are you doing?"

Travis grabbed the offered hand, getting and giving a traditional Texas firm handshake. Before saying anything, Frank flipped through the loan application he'd taken from Travis when he'd run into him in the bank lobby. "Good...at least helpful. I see a few thoughts I'll want to highlight. We've had a few successes, but the board seems to be less lenient recently."

Travis glanced around for a second or two before making his way closer, and Frank indicated they should head to his office so they could talk in private.

Travis sat down, followed by his loan officer. This time his throat tightened when the banker closed the door, sat behind his desk and said, "Well, Travis, let's see the rest of what you've got." He held his hand out for the envelope that was stuffed with the backup documentation Travis had been asked to provide. Frank put on a pair of reading glasses, brought out the material and spread everything over the desk. A few minutes into the process, Travis' leg had started shaking again. The waiting was wearing on his nerves.

Frank smiled. Travis hoped he wouldn't be grinning if he were delivering bad news. But this was the end of his search if he didn't get the money he needed today. He was hoping Frank would pass the application to the next level.

The review seemed like it was going as well as expected when Frank turned with an expression Travis couldn't interpret

"Everything's in order, so far as I can tell. You brought more than was asked for, in fact."

Travis grabbed at any chance to save his ranch. "I figured I should include any information that might be helpful."

Travis spent the rest of the hour reviewing everything with Frank and answering his questions. But on his trip home, he wasn't any more confident about the results. The drive back to the ranch seemed far longer than normal and provided little comfort.

Travis sat in his ranch office, staring out of the window to the expanse of drought-stricken land. At this point, he worried more about the phone call he was expecting from the banker than the condition of the ranch. Frank's news would dictate how Travis handled everything from here on out.

"Hey, buddy, how are things going?" Seth asked.

He turned to Seth and started drumming his fingers on the table. "Trying not to explode while I wait. You would think a hundred-year-old ranch would be worth the effort, and money, to save its operation for at least another generation. But from the way my bank's been acting, you would be wrong."

Seth nodded in understanding, giving Travis a visibly sympathetic ear. Now they were both in bad situations. Seth motioned to the empty chair in the room and asked, "You want some privacy? I would understand."

"No, please don't leave. I would like to have someone listening to me who has a little awareness of what I'm going through. I was hoping to talk to you while I waited for the phone call. Tell me about your day. It has to be better than how the money vulture of a banker made mine."

"Well, you remember the client who fired us the other day? The contact on our team who should be pleading the campaign to try to save it is an idiot — and the idiot who caused us to lose it. But now at least he's an unemployed idiot."

"Dave?"

"That's the one. You guessed him in one try. Unfortunately, he's the stereotype of someone working at an advertising agency — bloodthirsty and devoid of morals or tact."

Travis shook his head and made sympathetic noises. "Is it something you should discuss with the owner?"

"Well, for now I'll concentrate on saving my own job. Remember that Craig told me if I can get the client back, I can stay at the firm. The funny thing is that I wanted to lead the account from the beginning but just ended up as a co-team leader on it, thanks to Craig's forcing Dave on me. I even pitched a campaign against Dave's. So now I have the choice of saving the client or having my entire career come down because of a glass of root beer?"

Travis chuckled, shaking his head. "These days, nothing surprises me too much. I hope, at least, that if someone makes a living selling root beer in Texas, they have a sense of humor."

"Well, I thought they'd have someone with a sense of humor, but I guess I was wrong. The owners never liked Dave, and Craig didn't get that. You'd think a man who's been in advertising for years would be better at dealing with clients. But you would be wrong about my boss."

"How long do you have to pull off this miraculous turnaround?"

Seth started to answer when Travis' phone went off. He yanked it from his pocket, knowing who the call was from before he even looked.

He clicked the answer button then put the phone to his ear. "Frank, please tell me you have good news." The long pause from the caller told him all he needed to know. The bank would not be saving them. But he would force the banker to say the words. So, he stood without speaking, waiting for the banker to do his job.

"I'm sorry, Travis. I gave it my best to get you a loan. The board felt you were too close to bankruptcy to justify the loan you requested. Do you have questions?"

"Hell yes, but your answers won't make me happier. This is the end of the loan application, I assume?"

"I'm afraid it is…at least with these stipulations. The Board of Trustees made a unanimous decision to reject your loan. They offered one suggestion, but you won't like it."

"I don't see how I can get treated with even less dignity than a flat-out, unanimous no but go ahead. See if you can surprise me."

"If you would cut the ranch into small acreages for people who want to move into the country, they'll be happy to talk to you about an arrangement that would be very profitable for you."

"Oh, I was wrong. They can be more offensive than I thought." Travis lifted the phone and tapped the screen to break the connection. For several moments he sat feeling overwhelmed, but then he recalled Seth was sitting next to him. Besides, his dad had always said that real men didn't cry.

"Well, I guess that's one direction that doesn't show any possibility of saving the ranch." He repeated to Seth what all the banker had said.

"Do you have any other ideas?" Seth asked.

"That was my last one. How about you? Any suggestions you'd like my opinion about?"

Travis was surprised when he didn't get the response he'd expected from Seth. "Let me think about it. There might be something we could work with in the jerk's last suggestion about selling the land into chunks." He held up his hand to stall any argument from Travis. "I'm not talking about you selling the ranch, but we can identify some other things that your place is in a position to provide. Remember that you live close to one of the largest metroplexes in the country, and people like to be weekend cowboys."

"Okay, I'll keep my opinions to myself for now. Maybe you can come up with some ways to fund the ranch. Waiting a few more days won't hurt anything," Travis said. He rubbed his hands together. "I have a new herd-sire I'm checking out tomorrow. How would you like to take a trip to see a bull these guys are thinking I would like? The destination is about a hundred miles west of Fort Worth. Both of us could use a break from our normal weekend routine."

Seth leaned forward with a youthful expression. "I like that idea. I like it a lot."

Chapter Four

Seth rode without speaking as they drove through the mix of brush and grass that made up the landscape surrounding Wichita Falls. It wasn't what he'd expected. It wasn't a bad experience, just different. But the good thing was that he enjoyed the time he spent with Travis.

As they chatted, Travis became more relaxed. Seth enjoyed the sight of the sexy cowboy, from his tight-fitting Wranglers that left little to the imagination to his work-roughened hands and short, dark hair that was mostly covered by a light-colored cowboy hat Travis had informed him was proper summer wear. He had to laugh to himself because he was always giving Travis trouble about which century he lived in. It was a good-natured thing.

Travis was more than a working cowboy. He roped as a heeler and was good at it. Right now, the trip Seth was on with Travis was twofold. One reason was to go with him for company to the remote ranch where they were checking out a possible new herd-sire. The other was to see if there was some way to save Travis' family's land. Maybe if they could tap into a client base from the metroplex, the ranch might have the potential as a great tourist destination.

Seth licked his lips when Travis reached between his legs and adjusted his package. He'd had a couple of opportunities to view the goods hiding in the dark Wranglers. What they secreted inside got Seth's blood pressure rising.

"See anything that you're interested in sampling?" Travis asked with a grin.

Seth jumped a little at the accusation that he was checking Travis out—which he had been—but then Travis continued. "Shane and Dustin moved into this part of the country from West Texas. Every once in a while, they have an offspring from their herd that works as a rodeo bull, but that's not their goal. A focus of the breeding stock is raising grass-fed beef. But it says nothing about the herd's general disposition."

"What about the momma cows?"

"Most of them are as docile as an old Jersey milk cow, according to Shane." He paused and grew thoughtful. "But he did admit some of them would chase you into the pickup. Shane's got a bull now they thought would fit with our cows. This trip is to see if he's right."

Scary thoughts filled Seth's mind. "I had this picture—middle of nowhere, miles and miles between gas stations, basically a Texas version of *Deliverance*. But it is a nice time to get out of town and away from all the crap of last week. A Saturday buddy trip is a good thing."

"Several years ago they moved onto the new place where they are now. They seem to enjoy the solitude and distance from their neighbors," Travis said. "Both of them work in rodeo bull riding. You know Shane as a great bullfighter and Dustin was a world champion bull rider. They've diversified more than someone like me, who has to depend on his cattle's production to make a living. It's not much farther — well, twenty miles at the most. But it's a place anyone would be proud of. Dustin knows what he wants, and Shane has a rodeo school every once in a while. He told me he keeps his mind occupied dealing with young people who want to be bull riders."

They rode along a little farther, then Seth restarted the conversation.

Without sounding pitiful, he wanted to fill Travis in on what was happening in his life. "Well, it's only been a few days since 'the great upheaval', as we call it at the firm. I talked to Hank, the younger owner of the root beer factory, and floated a few ideas past him. At this point they're refusing to meet with the team, which I'm hoping will change. Dave torpedoed their account with the way he'd handled it. I could still strangle the asshole."

Travis reviewed the details. "The brand had a lot of time invested in it, but Dave destroyed the effort. That sucks, though. And it's not like you need more pressure."

"I should be at the house getting ready for a potential second presentation, but Amy will be there. She has plans with some girlfriends today, so there wouldn't be enough quiet for me to accomplish a thing." He turned to Travis and gave his best smile. "So, you have me — champion worrier, father and pole-bending instructor."

"No doubt about it. You could handle pole bending and barrel racing, even if you aren't a typical competitor in either of those competitions."

"Well, when your then-twelve-year-old falls in love with horses, you help her with the barrels and the pole bending for the Junior Rodeo...and you learn some things you never would've before."

They settled into a quiet thoughtfulness as they drove through the countryside for a good distance before passing what Seth would consider an old-fashioned country store. He popped Travis on the shoulder. "Hey, there's a little store. How about a bathroom break? And I could use a Coke too."

"I agree. Drain the snake and get a drink. Anything laced with caffeine and sugar would be wonderful."

Travis wheeled the pickup into one of the many empty parking places surrounding the store. They entered the business, and when they got back in the truck, he noticed something.

"What are you doing? Oh my God, are you putting peanuts in your Coke?"

"You bet, buddy. It's the best thing since sliced bread." Seth chuckled as he dumped the rest of a package of peanuts into his drink. He smacked his lips then swallowed some of the concoction. He picked up the bottle, took another drink and gazed at Travis. "You want to try some? It's good."

"No. I'll take your word for it. Right now I couldn't imagine anything could taste worse."

"Let me get this right. You'll eat salted caramel but you don't want to try peanuts in your pop, which has the same flavor profile?"

"You have it right. Salted caramel is delicious. That concoction is just nasty."

With a laugh and a shake of Seth's head, they settled into the truck and soon Travis was flying down the rural roads until they reached an ornate metal gate like something off South Fork on *Dallas*. Seth studied it for a few seconds before realizing that he did not understand how they're going to get in.

"Most ranches in the area have a security gate that people farther west wouldn't bother with. Dustin came up with this concept a few years ago. He created the metalwork and hired someone to install the electronics for him."

Travis punched in the code Dustin had given him earlier. He tried a few more times before hanging out of the window so he could push the enormous green button on the console and a distorted voice blared over the speaker. He had no idea what they'd said. Travis chuckled. "Let's give them a few minutes to make it work. I have seen Dustin down here cursing a blue streak at this contraption and threatening it with an eight-pound sledgehammer in the first days after they'd installed it. Once, Shane had them cut a hole in the wall to facilitate someone getting to the ranch headquarters when the electronic entrance was out."

Seth shook his head when the gate finally creaked open and Travis drove through the ornate metal construction. They made their way through a pastoral setting containing what Seth would consider the ugliest cattle he'd ever seen in his life. When he saw a cow nursing a yellow calf with dark tiger stripes over its shoulder, he had to wonder where the color cards had come from for the herd.

"I got my Beefmasters from them. They aren't the prettiest animals — well, at least not like classical beef breeds. They are a mix of several breeds over a hundred years. But at least part of their makeup comes from India, with the rest of the mix from the British Isles. Shane ensures me that this group of bulls is not something from a nightmare. Otherwise it will have been a long drive for nothing."

They pulled up at the headquarters, and before the truck stopped rolling, two guys stepped onto the porch. Travis shot his arm out and waved. "Shane! Dustin! It's good to see you, gentlemen. Hope everything is better here than it is at home." They got out and headed toward the house.

"We may have been luckier on the rainfall this year than you have. It's still been dry, though. But this country is more adapted to dry conditions than what you have around Dallas. But we're being rude hosts. I'm sure you're ready for something to drink."

Travis chuckled and waved his hand at Seth as they arrived at the porch. "Nothing for me, but this one has some kind of obsession with a nasty concoction of putting peanuts in his bottle of Coke."

Seth anticipated dissension from the other two, but he didn't get the response he was expecting.

"Coke and peanuts. It will go down in history as the ultimate comfort food for a ten-year-old boy who has been hauling hay all day," Shane said.

"Yeah, not many things give you the same buzz as Coke and peanuts on a July day."

Shane led them to the front door and opened it to a blast from the central air conditioner. Seth found a spot at the dining room table when they sat where cold air washed around him, giving the trio of friend's time to catch up on the gossip and recent news between the families. But soon they ended the traditional small talk and got down to business.

"I'm eager to hear your critical view of this bull. Hopefully, we won't have wasted your trip this morning."

"If it helps any, I gave him my field approval. If we wanted to build up some bucking stock, we would've kept him. Either way, he's a sweetheart," Dustin said.

Shane led them through the kitchen and out of the back door of the ranch house. After a quick stop in the mudroom where he and Dustin tugged on work boots, they tromped through the screen door. Behind the house was a maze of pens and buildings that Shane and Dustin had created, likely over time. They worked their way toward the pens where Seth spotted a bull. They stopped at an enclosure and leaned against the top metal rail, watching the animal inside for a few minutes.

The bull monitored their every move, even though it was young, and it seemed to have a second sense of everything going on around it. It had the hump on its shoulder like some bulls Zane had ridden. It seemed somewhat smaller, and its coloring wasn't as outlandish as some of the cattle they had seen on the ranch. He was cherry-red with a darker nose.

"That's it, baby. Figure out who we are. I bet they give you treats all the time." Travis winked at the ranchers. The bull walked around the enclosure like royalty. "We could name him Jackson. How would you like to be Jackson, big boy?"

The bull watched the people, keeping his distance.

After a few minutes, Shane turned to Travis. "Have I sold you a new herd bull?"

Seth had to say that it was a remarkable animal from his perspective. Zane had been on the top of so many bulls, but most of them had wanted to hurt him. Seth wasn't from a rural background and didn't know the finer points of what would appeal to Travis in making the decision.

Travis watched as the bull strutted around the small enclosure. His movements and red coloration were striking. If he were human, he'd be part of the gym-rat crowd. One of Shane's cattle dogs moved close to the fence, peering through the bars. This time the bull did not stay quiet.

It screamed and pawed chunks of earth into the air. Seth backed away from the fence, uncertain about how this would go.

Dustin watched it for a second before commenting. "Don't worry. He likes to mess with the bull, but the bull isn't that generous. If he ever catches that dog, it will be bloody. Nice choice of Jackson for his name. Weren't you using female characters from movies as names on your farm? So, Jackson would fit right in. He was one of the characters from *Fried Green Tomatoes*."

"The nice masculine name fits, except Jackson is from *Steel Magnolias*," Travis said.

Shane laughed and they started discussing a price, which didn't take long for them to work out. Shane offered to deliver the bull the following week.

They walked to the truck in a congenial mob. Travis seemed very comfortable with the way things were going. They shook hands, and Dustin gave both him and Travis a hug before they headed out.

Before long, Travis turned to Seth with a questioning glance. "What did you think of the bull?"

Seth considered the passing scenery for a few minutes then turn back to reply. "He seems muscular…you know, built. It didn't seem like he'd put up with crap from anybody, though."

Travis bobbed his head in agreement, "Yeah, that's the way I read it too. But if we handle him right, not with kid gloves or anything but right, he'll fit in."

They sped down the state highway, both lost in their thoughts. Seth started to say something when his phone rang. He dug in his pants pocket with a quizzical expression on his face.

"It's George with the root beer account. What the hell is he wanting on a Saturday afternoon?"

"Push the little green button, then you'll know," said Travis with a chuckle.

Seth gave himself a second, took a deep breath and let it out, then punched the button to answer his phone, putting the call on speaker.

"Hello, this is Seth. What can I do for you, George?"

A rumbling voice said, "Hank is with me too. We wanted to meet with you today."

Seth panicked. This could take up the rest of his day, and he was certain Travis would not appreciate his Saturday being destroyed.

Seth was frantically trying to think of how he could meet with the two men after he and Travis had finished their outing, but Travis squeezed his knee and got his attention. He looked over to catch him whispering, "Set up the meeting. No big deal."

Seth turned his focus back to the phone conversation. "I'm with a friend somewhere between Wichita Falls and Fort Worth, but I'd be happy to help you any way I can. What were you thinking?"

The voice he heard this time was the younger of the two men. "We were talking about the pitch that your firm made for our company and how it didn't fit what we wanted. But we want you guys to get a real chance at it."

George took over the conversation again. "We figured out the other guy didn't understand what we sold. You people were envisioning something that might have worked when I first opened the company twenty years ago, but that's outdated. We don't sell grilled cheese sandwiches and tomato soup over the counter. We formulate craft root beer concentrate and resell it to the commercial industry, which is a much bigger portion of our market than any mom-and-pop restaurants who might sell root beer on one of their taps. We're also real interested in a specialty market too, something fitting with the craft beer craze and foodie demands."

Seth nodded, beginning to get where they'd gone wrong. "I understand what you're talking about. I can work that into the proposal for Monday if you'd like."

George exploded over the phone. "*Hell* no! We're not calling to add something to another time-wasting meeting in your office. We want you to come here— today—to see what it is we do."

Seth could feel the panic settle into his system. "George, like I said, I'm with a friend of mine. I would have to—" But Travis was motioning for Seth to take care of his client. Travis had even managed to pull into a roadside rest area.

Travis reached over to put Seth's phone on hold then whispered, "I can wait in the pickup and work from the phone even. Go ahead. Set up your tour." Travis chuckled. "I might even get a root beer float out of them. I'm sure they have stuff for visitors to try out."

"Okay, George. We're about an hour from your facility. Is that where you want to meet?"

"That would be great. We'll get this straightened out. Hank and I will meet you here afterwhile."

The phone went dead. Seth lifted it away and scanned it to confirm that George had hung up.

He turned to Travis with a grimace on his face. "Sorry about this. I didn't mean to get you involved in the great root beer caper."

Travis chuckled and gave Seth an affectionate pat on the shoulder. "It's no big deal. I can take care of some things on the phone. I've done it before. It's only fair that I get to do this for a friend."

"Well let's head out. Their factory's on the west edge of Fort Worth, so we should get there in a little less than an hour if traffic isn't too bad."

About an hour later they rolled into the parking lot of an industrial complex.

Seth realized he was as guilty as Dave in that he had never come here to view the operation. Now that he was being called on the carpet, he wasn't sure how this meeting would play out.

Oh well, Craig will just have to understand.

But it was the only means he saw of them getting the client back. As he turned to Travis, he realized two figures had exited the building and were moving toward them.

"Oh crap, they're coming. I don't see how this can be a good thing."

"It's like a private tour of the factory," said Travis. "I may get my root beer float after all."

Once the executives got closer, Hank motioned for them to follow him and led them into an ornately decorated conference room. George moved to the end of the table while the others sat opposite him. Seth wanted to make certain they understood his friend's presence. "This is Travis Davis, a friend of mine. Our kids rodeo together. I was with him today searching for a new herd bull for his ranch, so he got drafted into this side trip."

Hank smiled at the pair. "A fresh perspective might be good."

Travis grinned at the other two. "I love Hill Country root beer. It's my favorite…with vanilla ice cream. Your batches of craft drinks, from what I can remember, were amazing. I'll look forward to a sampling at the end of the tour."

Hank scowled at his father. "I told you we needed a tasting room. It could be a tourist destination for the area. See the reaction Travis had?"

George's expression turned sour. "I'm not so sure, but why don't you get him a sample from the icebox?"

Hank was only gone for a few minutes before he was back sporting a huge root beer float, which he handed to Travis. He took a tentative first sip then a grin covered his face.

Seth smiled at the enthusiasm Travis was displaying for the float as the conversation began, remaining on small talk in the beginning. They'd get to the meat of the issue before long, Seth was sure.

Travis soon finished his float, making them all laugh as he intentionally made sucking noises with his straw to show them that he wasn't going to leave a single drop of his delicious treat. "That was the best I've had in a long time. Do you have other flavors?"

"Sure, we have a mix of old fashion flavors like sassafras, sarsaparilla and several of cream sodas — what you'd call nostalgia tastes. Those are all new lines."

With that information, details came into focus for Seth. "So, these expanded and unusual formulas are the ones you want campaigns created around?"

Hank beamed at Seth, popped open a bottle and handed it to him. "That was why we came to your firm."

George turned to Travis. "I would appreciate your opinion as we go through this. We want to expand several of our lines, as you can see, and add a new one—Pearl River Creme Soda. To help you to understand our market, most of our customers grew up in Dallas, or someplace similar, and never had the experience of the local country store." He paused for a moment before washing a huge smile over them. "And we're done telling you about it. We need to show Seth what we want to do."

With that, the owners began their tour, pointing things out as they went but still sharing their vision of what they wanted from Seth.

"We will represent the brand using the local hamburger stand look, the kind of place where you meet your friends after the Friday night football game. You know the type? We've been exchanging emails, but so far the previous contact didn't seem to get us," Hank said.

That gave Seth his next clue as to why they had lost the account. Dave had never paid attention to the information that they'd sent. He probably thought this was a little mom-and-pop operation that had no business being out in the corporate world. He couldn't have been more wrong. Then Seth realized Travis was talking with the owners.

"Your root beer is the best. I could spend the evening drinking it, go to bed, get up and start again. You guys will be doing a great service for this region when you start adding to the existing lines."

"We're gonna have some new flavors, things like tropical mango and Texas raspberry, but everything works together. We're going to keep our taste testers busy," Hank said.

Travis was doing what Seth considered a brilliant job of chatting up the client. It was a shame he couldn't have Travis make the owner feel comfortable with their advertising team. That was one thing Seth felt he could have done better, but Travis was obviously a gifted salesman.

"You've got quite a selection now," Travis told the owners. "I bet you're filled with some great ideas on what you should do to promote them. It's a perfect combination."

They made it back to the conference room and sat.

Seth was going over his notes and making more. He wanted to make sure he missed nothing this time. But when he glanced up, Travis gave him a wink.

"You know the sample was fantastic. Too bad I couldn't get some of all the flavors. We could share samples with the team." Travis winked again. "Yep, it's a shame. It would show Seth's group that taste of summer I remember so well from my childhood."

Seth took up at Travis' prompt. "Have you considered creating just that? It might be a new market, making frozen treats."

"Well, I guess. Hmm-m." George collected his thoughts. "I suppose it's something we could talk about..."

Hank had disappeared while they had been talking with George. As they were wrapping up the session on how things would proceed, Hank appeared with a handcart filled with cartons of their drinks. He filled the counter with every kind of beverage they'd been making since George had started the business. Hank set down the last six-pack and grinned.

"I thought this might be helpful. What kind of ideas can you come up with? These should give you a starting point."

George glanced around the room then gave the first genuine smile Seth had seen from the older man. "This was productive—much more so than sitting in your glass-walled offices listening to people who didn't understand what they were talking about."

Seth's face heated at the accusations, but he couldn't disagree with what they were saying.

"That's all behind us...ancient history. Now with the new product line defined, my man here has great ideas on how to market your company," said Travis.

"You bet. And the samples will come in handy," Seth agreed.

They exchanged firm handshakes before loading into the pick-up for the trip home. Once they were out of sight of the factory, Seth let out a huge breath he'd felt like he been holding since they'd arrived. He turned to Travis and smiled.

"When did you become the super salesman?"

* * * *

Travis stood in the doorway and let his eyes adjust to the dim interior. After a few seconds, he could make out individual shapes inside. Moreover, he heard the murmur of voices on the other side of the stalls.

He recognized the people speaking and smiled to himself. It was James and Troy. They worked on the ranch. James had lived there since Travis had been a kid, and Troy had been born there. They were a father and son pair who Travis did not want to lose in the current turmoil.

"Hey, guys. How's everything this morning?" Travis asked.

They jumped a bit at the intrusion, and James looked a little guilty.

"Hey, boss, we were just taking a break so I can check in on what's happening with Troy. You know, the normal father son things to talk about in a fifteen-minute break." James laughed.

Travis had to think for a minute. How old was Troy? He still seemed like that kid who followed James around nonstop. His tiny shadow. But now Travis realized it wouldn't be long before Troy finished high school. There would be a pickup, dating then off to college.

"So, the typical goals? Get rich and retire to the Bahamas?" Travis smiled at the teen.

"Hey, Travis, that sounds like a good idea. Can you give me a hookup up with the wealthy teenager's club? I'd be good with that."

James cringed, likely a bit embarrassed by the casual familiarity from Troy in speaking with his dad's employer.

Travis knew the next words out of James' mouth would be to tell his son to be respectful of his elders. But he was okay with the level of informality Troy was using. He cut his eyes over and motioned to James. There was a moment of tension then the man relaxed.

Travis refocused his attention on Troy. "I'm afraid you're at the wrong place if you're wanting to be rich. I can't even get the banker to loan me money for a few loads of hay from Nebraska. But if you figure out how to move into 'the wealthy rancher' category, let me know. And if you have any suggestions for how to keep this place afloat for the next few years, be sure and let me know that too."

Travis was teasing the young man, but though Troy hesitated, he held his ground.

"Dad and I were just talking about other duties for me to earn money. It doesn't seem to grow on trees around this area."

"What ideas did y'all come up with?" Travis asked. "Because you're right. This is a tough place to find a job for anybody, especially high school students."

"Rodeo. I'm old enough. I could've started several years ago. But if I work at it and Dad puts some money back, maybe I could do what Zane's trying to accomplish. With the scholarship to A&M or Texas Tech, I could go to school. I need to consider a major. I love the ranch, but it can only support so many generations of families. So, Dad and I realized a scholarship was the best way for me to reach my goals."

This time Travis said nothing but gazed back and forth between the father and son. But after a short time, Travis asked, "So, what part of rodeo could we help with?"

Troy glanced around, took a breath then put all his focus back on Travis. "I was thinking about that, to be honest. We can't afford a horse or the place to keep it. And while bronc riding is not as glamorous as bull riding, not as many bronc riders get hurt. I'm still looking at my options."

Travis considered what he'd said. "It wouldn't take much to make you more competitive on either event. We might help you with some pointers too. Lord knows that Zane and I spent enough time together, especially in the beginning."

He considered for a moment, tapping his fingers on the railing surrounding the arena. He began to work through his thoughts. "There are a couple of things you might not have looked at. We're already set up to help someone wanting to be a bull rider. What with Zane coming out almost every day, adding a few more bulls to the list wouldn't strain the resources. Your thinking is sound, Troy. Horses get expensive. You see what we have around when Amy competes. But that also means we have some of the equipment you would need if you wanted to try bronc riding, which brings me to another point. You're right about the bull riding being more glamorous, but have you regarded the facilities we have here on the ranch?"

He studied Travis for a few seconds before replying. "What do you mean, Mr. Davis? Dad and I don't want to do anything that will make life more difficult for you and Amy."

Travis gave him a dismissive wave. "No problem at all, son. Zane is already here most mornings to practice. We could add another bull or two to keep an extra for you. And the bull riding no doubt has more glamour and cash." Travis laughed softly.

"No, boss, we don't want you to do anything special for Troy. College is so dang expensive these days. We have to find something other than student loans for him to fund his schooling."

Travis scowled at James. "Now, if you keep up that talk, you *will* piss me off. You and Troy are family. Anything I can do to help, I will. Getting a couple of bigger bulls to make it easier for you and Zane to practice on would not be that difficult."

"Travis, we don't think you have some kind of endless resources. It's not like I'm turning down your assistance. I just don't want to feel like we are taking advantage of you."

"Keep working on the details and find plans we can make work. But a bull rider from here wouldn't hurt our promotion. We might even sell some bulls who are ready to start to a stock contractor." Travis studied the pens for a minute. "So, Troy, you say you haven't ridden a bull before?"

"No, sir. It just didn't seem appropriate for me to sneak rides on some of the ranch stock."

Travis nodded in understanding and beamed at the kid. "We have one yearling that had come up with a cut on its shoulder. He's fine now and ready to go back into the paddocks. But we could keep him up here longer, let you practice and get the flavor for the event. I know enough about the equipment to get you on and buckled up for your first ride."

"You would be okay with that?" Troy asked.

They both turn to James, who had become somewhat green. But Travis had given James a way to try out Troy's dream, all without him needing to lift a finger or spend a dime.

While they had been having the discussion, Seth and Zane arrived for Zane to practice.

"Yeah. This should let you try it so you can see if you want to do this or not," James finally said.

As they were working out the details, the group walked to the arena. They went to the fence surrounding the grounds to see the yearling Travis had been talking about.

"This is the bull that had the injury. I thought he'd be a good one for Troy to try out before we send him back to the herd," Travis explained to Seth and Zane.

"So, we can set up a run and let him have a taste of the sport?" James confirmed the idea.

"Yeah, that's a great idea." Zane turned to Troy. "It might take more than just one run to decide if you want to deal with bull riding, though. The good news is I can help you with the rigging, which looks easy but is a pain in the ass."

"Zane! Your language," Seth said.

Zane leaned on the rail. "Do you think that's the worst he's heard before?" Zane gave Troy a wink.

Seth popped Zane across the back of his head. "I don't want my son to be the one that teaches him."

"Don't worry, Travis. I've heard much worse. You should hear Dad when he smashes his finger." The crowd laughed as James turned crimson red. The expression he shot Troy left no doubt that they would discuss that later.

Troy gave Zane a worshiping glance then said, "I want to try it. Dad and Travis have all this stuff, but I don't know what half of it is. And I don't know how to put on any of it...and what goes on the bull and what goes on me."

Zane looked over everything then began to explain. "Well, this is your helmet and protective vest. Dad still makes me wear them." He turned aside and gave Seth a wink of conspiracy. "It keeps my brains from being spread all over an arena."

Travis smiled at James. "Since Zane's here to help, let's get him on a bull for a test run right now. He'll either fall in love with it or hate it. The adrenalin surge is amazing."

Travis could tell that Troy's nerves were getting the best of him, but then, if he wasn't nervous, Travis would've been concerned. The bull he was riding was being calm, at least for now, but he should have enough power and a raw ability to get the adrenaline of a fourteen-year-old boy flowing.

"Troy, come over here for a second. Seth and Zane will get you into safety gear." Troy stood with only a slight amount of shaking while they dug through some of Zane's old equipment. If any of the gear fit Troy, he was welcome to it. Zane had not been that small in years.

"Let's get you ready to give this a try." Seth went with Zane to get Troy dressed.

A few minutes later Travis realized he wasn't needed at this end of the ride but might help get the animal ready.

Travis left the tack room, moved to the arena and helped James put on the bull's equipment. Travis reviewed everything, confirming it was all exactly where and how it should be.

He shifted his attention to Troy when he appeared. "So, what do you think? Still want to give it a try? There's no shame in saying you don't."

Troy stood for an instant then locked eyes with Travis. "I'm ready. This is gonna be the beginning of something new for me — and it'll be great."

Travis glanced at James, wanting to know how the dad was doing in this whole process. When James gave him a quick nod, he knew the time had come.

"James, you'll want to sit over in the bleachers so you can record this for posterity." Travis chuckled before he continued. "Seth and I will be the bullfighters. I don't think this guy will run anybody down, but you never know. Zane, you can open the gate."

Within a few minutes everyone had moved to their position. Troy was in the chute with his hand laced through the rope that was situated in the middle of the bull's back. Travis caught his attention. "Whenever you're ready, Troy, nod your head. Zane will open the gate. The bull will run, but you'll get a few good bucks."

It was obvious Troy was fighting a bad case of nerves, justifiable so far as Travis was concerned. Then it happened... Troy nodded his head, Zane snapped open the section of fence that made up the chute and the bull started a bucking run.

Well, crap.

He motioned to Seth and the two of them tried to converge on the suddenly now-motionless bull.

"Give him a little nudge with the heel of your boots. You need to encourage him to move. He's got to move," yelled Travis.

Troy was nodding like crazy and running the heels of his boots down the bull's muscular shoulders. This time when they challenged the bull, it ducked his head between its front legs, curled up like a C and started to buck.

About half a second later, Travis realized he'd forgotten to start the stopwatch, but he'd sat through enough eight-second events in his life that he should be able to time this run with no help from a mechanical device.

The bull was tearing up the ground of the arena, but Troy was still on his back. After a few more seconds, Travis decided they had gone long enough.

"That's it...eight seconds."

At that point, the bull started spinning, swapping end for end, like the big boys from a stock contractor. It thrilled Travis to see how well Troy did on his first try but then he realized the fourteen-year-old couldn't let go.

"Seth, we need to help Troy. He can't get his hand loose from the gear."

A few more seconds without any progress getting Troy loose and James was on his way to rescue his son.

He and Seth ran at the bull at the same time. But to his surprise, the animal paused for a split second. Troy popped loose and landed on his butt in the dirt. Most people would consider it a successful dismount. No one got hurt.

Within a few seconds, everyone surrounded Troy to hear his opinion of the experience and check on his condition. Travis waited until he thought he might burst with excitement before asking, "Well? What did you think, Troy?"

A brilliant smile appeared against his dust-coated face. "Can I ride again? Maybe a bigger bull?"

Chapter Five

Seth searched the room and gathered everything needed for the day's meeting into his leather messenger bag. He'd spent the entire week working on the Hill Country Root Beer client campaign. He felt like he had it under control, and George and Hank even seemed pleased with the direction things were going.

I wish I could get the two of them to Facetime with me. Then I could touch base on minor questions. But that's for another day, another battle.

He checked the clothing he was wearing. He wanted to be certain it worked for today's meeting, a good combination of professional and rural. Zane walked through the door munching on a cinnamon roll.

"Who are you getting all pretty for? Seems like a waste of time to me. A few years ago, you worked in jeans and polo shirts," Zane said.

"Well, today is the day I present to the client who fired us a few days ago. You know...the one who decides whether I have a job tomorrow," Seth said with more than a little note of sarcasm.

Zane froze with the final bite of food halfway to his mouth. He had the good graces to look somewhat abashed when their eyes met. "Oh. I understand how you might be tense."

Seth brushed the imagined bits of lint from his pants and turned to Zane. "I picked up some enchiladas. Follow the instructions on the container to heat them up if you get hungry. A bowl of salad is in there too. But don't eat too much because this won't be supper. We're going out to celebrate the successful campaign launch. What do you think of steak at Mesquite Grill?"

Zane said, "Okay. Sure. I can handle that. Right now I need to dress and get over to the ranch. I promised Troy to go over some tips on how to get the riding gear on a stubborn bull. Little Bit is getting to be more than Troy wants to deal with by himself." Zane chuckled around a mouthful of food.

Seth stopped for a minute and studied his son. "Is he still safe? I don't want someone hurt when the two of you are screwing around."

"It'll be fine. Travis is helping us too." Zane cocked his head and gave Seth a quizzical gaze. "You know that he understands a lot more about rodeo than we give him credit for. I mean, I always knew he was researching pole bending and the barrels for Amy, but he's darn good with all the different events. I realized he has given me a bunch of good pointers over the years, and some were fantastic."

"Travis is a sharp guy. It wouldn't hurt any of us to listen to him. If only I could discover some way to help him save the ranch."

"Yeah, me too. So far I haven't come up with anything I think might work." Zane shrugged. "I don't know, but if we can find something to tap into what a good teacher he is, that might be exciting. But I guess you can't make a living teaching people how to compete in rodeo events."

Seth felt like someone had just hit him between the eyes with a hammer. "Why not? I mean, we could have all kinds of things at the ranch that would make money. Something like one of those trendy farms-to-table events might not be bad either. But I think he could tap into the fact that we live so close to a few major Texas cities." Seth gathered the last of his materials and headed out of the door. "But for now, I need to save our bacon—because my son seems to think he needs a side of beef a day for his high-protein regimen."

"It doesn't have to be beef. Any meat will do…even chicken."

Seth rushed out, hoping he was wrong about how long this trip was going to take this morning. The amount of time it took to get through the Dallas rush-hour traffic and to his office was always questionable. He wouldn't get much sympathy from George and Hank, either, because they were farther away. But regardless, he had the campaign nailed down. It had to be the perfect mix of old-fashioned nostalgia and contemporary foodie. Hill Country might even start their own brick-and-mortar store, he'd learned. Before any of that happened, though, Seth had to get through the day without something causing the presentation to crater. He started his car, enjoying the low rumble of the engine before he slipped it into gear and started out.

The time passed quickly as Seth continued reviewing the campaign's details, and the traffic wasn't nearly as bad as he'd experienced before.

An hour later found Seth standing before the company's double glass doors staring at the simple notices taped to both of them. He read them carefully as his life collapsed. They represented the culmination of a week of horrible days that Seth didn't know how to process. He traced his finger down the notice on the door that was locked, but the desperation didn't change. He couldn't make it lessen as he read the message again. The agency was declaring bankruptcy and liquidating assets. The accountants would distribute final paychecks once they had made the needed adjustments.

The rest of what was on the announcement was legal gibberish. His frustration became overwhelming until Seth wanted to pound against the thick glass again, not sure what he could do at this point.

"If it would help, we could commiserate together."

A lot of things were happening, but the visage he saw when he turned to see who had spoken was among the most shocking. He gathered his thoughts. "Hey? I thought you'd left the firm."

Dave shrugged and nodded at the announcement. "This was Craig's final triumph. I was at the office yesterday to beg for my job again, and now I find he has closed the agency. What an ass. I begged for my job and gave such a great performance—and now I'm unemployed."

"Well that's crappy, but he always played people," Seth said.

"You think? A little difficult? Will give you extra work for management skills… Yeah, right."

"I have clients coming to see the presentation that I have ready and now there is no firm. How could I have been such a dumbass?" He turned to glare at Dave. "It's the Hill Country Root Beer client, by the way. You never even went to see their facilities. They have a slick operation with a lot of innovation."

Dave sighed, again dropping his fist against the glass door in one last futile gesture.

Seth finally said, "Standing here and pointing out what an ass Craig was will not help with anything this morning. I have to go see what I'll do with the house and a kid who thinks he's going to college."

"Maybe it won't be as bad as you think. You must have other options."

"You'd think so," Seth said. "I guess I'll go home and see what they look like."

Just as he was getting in his car to leave, Hank and his father pulled into the parking lot. Seth's heart sank but he steeled himself to do what he's had to do. He watched as the pair headed directly to him. Obviously, they could tell something was wrong. Once they were close enough to be within easy speaking distance, Hank motioned over his shoulder toward the old office building.

"I guess this isn't some kind of innovative way of telling us to get with the times?" Hank said.

Seth dropped his head and shook it a little. "I think it's a big 'fuck you' to all of us. The notice on the door does say the accountants will be working on the paperwork to refund everyone's money — or something along those lines."

Hank gave him a sympathetic expression then shrugged. "Other than making a special trip to Fort Worth, it didn't change much of our plans. "

"It's too bad they're going out of business. We've been talking about it and decided we could work with your firm. It sounds like Craig has taken any chance of that happening and shot it in the ass."

Seth didn't know what to say. Nothing really covered the situation. So, he decided he had nothing to lose, regardless of what he said, so he'd go with the truth. He turned to face the two of them. "I'm really sorry things turned out the way they did. I have no idea what happened. All of the employees are as in the dark as you are."

He stood around for the next few minutes, trying to carry on a conversation with some of the other employees, but everything only became darker the more they had time to think about it. None of the conversation was improving the situation.

He realized George and Hank had not left, so he tried to pull together something to put some closure to the situation.

"I wish I could give you more details. I will pass along anything I find out so you know what's going on too. I can't tell you how sorry I am about this, but I don't know what else I can do." There were reassurances passed between Seth and his clients, but there was nothing else he could add. When it became obvious that Seth had no more information, Hank and George returned to their vehicle and left.

Seth sat in his car for quite some time, struggling to put his thoughts together. Then without much contemplation or reason, he drove out of the parking garage and drove north. That was the last rational thought he had for quite some time.

When his thoughts started to return into a cohesive mass, he found himself pulling into the driveway leading to Travis' ranch. In part he wanted to scream and curse. *Why do I keep coming back to Travis each time there is some problem?* It really wasn't fair to his friend, but Seth wasn't quite sure it was fair to him either.

He sat staring at the scene before him, knowing he couldn't turn around and leave at this point. Somebody would have noticed him and he would have to explain to Travis why he'd been there and not gotten out of his car. *As if I knew what was going on.* Seth gave himself a few additional minutes to gather his thoughts, opened the door and stepped out.

This time he didn't find a Travis who was spewing profanity. It actually took a few minutes because Travis was quietly working with one of the horses. Seth thought it was one of Amy's horses from years before but he wasn't certain. Regardless, he'd come here for a reason, even if he didn't have a clue what he was going to say.

Travis glanced over and smiled, giving Seth a little wave as he continued to handle the horse. Then he started going over the mare with a fine brush, which seemed to calm her. To Seth's amusement, it was having the same effect on him. Travis moved around the mare and gave Seth a wink. "She's calming down. She was one spastic animal, wouldn't let Amy anywhere close. She even tried the stunt with me a few times, but it didn't do her any good."

Travis stood without speaking, running his hand over the horse's head to let her breathe in his scent. Seth watch for several minutes, not saying anything, just enjoying the time with a man he considered handsome and his friend.

"Do you want to tell me what's wrong?" Travis asked.

"What makes you think there is a problem?"

"Mostly the expression on your face. It's the same one you get every time you're trying to work out a problem by yourself when you need help."

Seth started to argue with him and realized he was right. "Problems at work, serious shit."

"Damn, it's like pulling teeth to get anything out of you. What happened?" Travis asked.

"Craig shut down the firm. He didn't give anyone any warning. The place is locked up. Everyone lost their job."

"Oh, no. What happened, Seth? I'm so sorry."

Seth slumped as the weight of the day washed over him. He looked at Travis. "I had no idea. When I got to work this morning, there were notices plastered over the locked entry doors. There was no real explanation, though."

"What about the guys you were meeting? Wasn't it important?"

He motioned at Travis. "Yeah, it was the Hill Country guys. I'm sure they would be happy to have you visit them again. Unlike everyone else, they liked you last time. But I told them there won't be any more meetings, not with that firm anyway. Now all I have to do is find new housing. Hopefully we don't end up living in a trailer park on the edge of Tyler."

Travis immediately said, "You can live here. There's no way I'm going to let you stay in some rental. It's more convenient for the two of you anyway. Zane can finish high school without having to transfer. We've got three bedrooms and two bathrooms. That leaves a room each for Zane and Amy. The two of us could share the main bedroom." Travis studied Seth then asked, "How does that sound? No, it's not as good as where you were living, but it's a roof over your head and food on the table until you get back to your life."

"Travis, it's too much. And I can't impose that way. You have your own life to live, and the ranch is struggling.

"It won't be that big of a deal," said Travis. "With all the summer rodeos, you're here most of the time anyway." He gave a laugh.

"I don't think it would be fair. We aren't cheap to keep. It will take a while to get my unemployment check or the money from the firm, and I don't know how long before either of them shows up."

Travis paused for a few seconds before continuing. "It's not gonna change anything, and you can just stop arguing with me. If there's some big problem, we'll deal with it. We've been traveling together for years and we have dealt with a lot of crap... Without having a meltdown, do you see how any of this is really changing us? If anything, it'll make it easier for us to get to the events on time. We can divide and conquer.

"It sounds like a workable solution, I guess. I can't tell you how much I appreciate it. But I have to be honest. Without a salary, I don't have extra to pay you each month. Mary's treatments wiped out our savings."

Travis waved his hand. "Don't be ridiculous. I'm not asking for rent. You can use whatever is here to help you get on your feet again, to give yourself time to decide what you want. Isn't that how you ended up working for Craig in the first place? Got into a big hurry and ended up at a firm that was flaky as hell?"

Seth considered before nodding. "Yeah, you have a good point. But I don't want you to think I'm being a lazy ass and mooching off of you."

"Let's have a glass of sweet tea and calm down a bit. When you're ready, we can decide how to get you some drawers in the bedroom for your stuff. If you're living here, it will be easier for you to get your house ready to sell and get it onto the market."

Seth was speechless as he was walked into the house. They went to the kitchen, where Travis gave Seth a huge tumbler of sweet iced tea. Although he would have to break it to Travis at some point, he wasn't a huge fan of sweet tea. Travis, on the other hand, was happiest with a glass of it in his hand at all times.

He realized Travis was waiting on a response from him. "Sorry, man. What did you ask?"

"I was repeating that we only have one bathroom to share between the two of us. Hope that won't be a problem."

Seth considered the possibility of seeing his buddy's naked body every morning and the thought left him with a growing erection. "It will be fine. I'm sure we can work out all the details. I think your morning routine starts earlier than mine," said Seth. He grabbed Travis' arm. "Look... I know you're saying everything is going to be fine. And I see where that's coming from, but I worry that we're imposing on you and Amy. Some parts of this are going to be harder than others, like sharing a bed. That seems like something a lot more important than a sleepover when you're twelve. I know you're going to make it easy for us, but I have concerns. You know you're a hot-looking guy, you know I'd like to take our friendship to the next level and that things were a lot different when we made the agreement... I'd think we're going to need to talk about it again. Don't you?"

Travis paused and studied Seth for a few seconds before motioning him to follow to a cluster of chairs they had included on the new front porch. Travis indicated one of the chairs then seemed to lose himself in the sky above them.

Time stretched until the silence wore on Seth, then Travis leaned forward and spoke at a low tone. "Maybe you aren't the only one who's been considering that agreement we made."

"What? Y-You? You've got to be fucking k-kidding me," Seth managed to stammer.

Travis continued, "I've been thinking about it since you said something after that massage. Here's my suggestion. We both want to explore a new experience, but it doesn't have to be right now. I think we both have enough going on without adding anymore changes to our lives. So, you and Zane get the stuff you need to move in right now. That will give you time to get your house ready to sell right away so you won't lose it. Just bring over the bare minimum that you need for now. We can get the rest later. You know where Zane's room will be and I'll have space cleared out for your stuff in the master bedroom. Amy is at some student meeting and I'm going to check the calves once I get the spaces emptied, but we can both help you once we are back. If you need anything, let me know."

Travis turned with a smile and headed back into the house.

It was just as well that Travis had gone before Seth could say anything because he was speechless. *He wants more, too? And we're going to share a bed* and *a bathroom?*

* * * *

Seth was making breakfast for them all using the outdoor kitchen Travis had installed a few years earlier. Cooking had become one of the chores Seth had always gravitated toward, and in the short time he and Zane had been there, he'd taken it on to ease Travis' burden. Today his main task was to let everyone know when Shane and Dustin arrived with the new herd bull.

Seth made a quick trip to the kitchen and heard noises coming from the bedroom. It was getting much easier to call it 'their bedroom'. In spite of that, he refocused on his cooking. He layered the bottom of a heavy cast-iron skillet with thick applewood smoked bacon that perfumed the temperate breeze playing across the patio. While cooking for the group, he lost track of time, and by the time he'd cracked the eggs into the bubbling bacon grease, Travis had found his way to Seth's side.

"You know, I can get used to someone making me breakfast every morning."

Seth shrugged but shot him a grin. "Yeah, I wanted to make sure I included the owner of the ranch."

Travis sat in a chair clad only in his briefs and a T-shirt, but that was normal. Seth would not parade around in his underwear in front of Amy. He'd told Zane it wasn't acceptable for any man not her father to walk around in nothing but his skivvies. Shorts and T-shirts were fine though.

The brilliant orange-yolked eggs he'd gathered the day before were turning white around their perimeter. The farm-fresh eggs were just one of the things that Seth found amazing about his new living arrangement.

Seth added a generous amount of home fries and a few strips of bacon to a plate. He set it down in front of

Travis with a smile. "Biscuits are almost ready, a couple more minutes. But dig in while the food is hot."

Seth knew Amy and Zane would be stumbling out soon. He'd layered their rooms with more than one chiming alarm. They wouldn't be happy, maybe, but they'd be up.

He worked until the timer went off, getting the steaming biscuits out of the oven, filling Zane's and Amy's plates and putting them on the table. They would eat whenever they finished getting ready, which should be about now.

"Biscuits are ready. I have plates made for both kids, and there's plenty of food left if you want seconds, including an entire sheet of homemade biscuits resting on the stove. You've seen Zane eat. He'll lick the plates clean."

"You will have us packing on the pounds. At worst, we'll be too heavy for horses to hold," Travis said.

Seth enjoyed the accolades for his simple breakfast. He took a minute to check on everything before finding a place to sit. He bit into the potatoes and nodded his head. "Wow, this is good. I was never sure about the farm-to-table and farmers' market culture, but everything tastes delicious and is *so* fresh."

Travis was ready for a second helping. Seth saw him move, jumped up and was filling Travis' plate as soon as he started to stand. "Here. I've got more. Don't forget the pan of homemade buttermilk biscuits. Stick some bacon on it, and they'll keep for a midmorning snack."

Travis glanced at Seth but didn't complain when his plate was filled a second time. He heard the shuffle of people coming through the house on their way to the outdoor kitchen and he sat back down. Zane and Amy stumbled onto the patio, wiping the sleep from their eyes and giving him the side-eye. *Ah, so my alarms worked!* Seth grabbed their plates and put them on the table as he motioned them to sit down. He got the gallon of milk from the refrigerator and poured them something to drink.

Travis pushed his empty plate away and took a sip of the piping hot coffee that Seth had set beside him a few seconds earlier.

"Excellent. A great breakfast, Seth. We appreciate it." He waved to the two teenagers who were eating like they hadn't seen food in a month. "Is that right, kids? Zane, your dad's doing a bang-up job."

The two youngsters managed small smiles between bites, which was about as much communication as Seth thought he'd get after his alarm caper.

The breakfast plates were emptied in a flurry and the kids scattered to do the morning chores and get in a few practice rounds. Travis emerged for work, his Wranglers molded in place. He popped his hat off the rack by the front door, put it on and turned to Seth.

"You remember that Shane is delivering Jackson today. We finished repairing the pens, so he'll be fine. I'm running to Mesquite and picking up parts at the John Deere dealership for the new problems with the equipment that broke yesterday. One of the small hay meadows has enough standing grass to harvest, and that will give us some space to breathe. I'm not sure what you want to do, but you could run into town with me or have some time to yourself."

"What if I stay here and help Shane? That would save you some time. It doesn't feel like rain to me, but with our luck, it will pour as soon as you have any hay on the ground."

The tension drained from Travis as he shot Seth a grin. "That would be great. You don't have to do much to help. Just make sure we have everything locked up so Jackson isn't visiting with any girl who might get in the mood."

Seth laughed and flipped the towel over his shoulder, signaling the end of breakfast. "I'll get dressed. I'm betting Shane doesn't sleep late and neither does his partner."

"Husband."

"What?"

"Dustin is Shane's husband. They got married four years back. I think it's part of the reason they moved closer to civilization. Although I wouldn't call Wichita Falls a cultural hub of west Texas, and Lord knows, they are still way out in the country."

"Duly noted. I'll be careful. I don't want to offend any friends we might have."

"Oh, I don't think you would piss off either of them. It's obvious they're a couple, regardless."

Seth was finishing up the last details they were using to keep the new bull under control for his first few days on the ranch. It was not a lot to do. Keep him watered in the heat, fill the hay feeder — standard stuff. He lifted the last pile of old bedding into the wheelbarrow when he heard the roar of a diesel engine coming up the driveway.

Seth quickly moved his equipment to one side, clearing the way. The unloading chute was ready. All they had to do was back the trailer to it, get everything lined up and open the gate. It would be that simple. He walked around the truck to the open window to greet Shane, but it wasn't Shane behind the wheel grinning at him. It was Dustin.

"So, you drew the short straw today too?" Dustin said.

Seth was confused. "Short straw? What do you mean?"

"You mean to tell me you haven't ever heard of someone getting the short straw for something? It's when you're doing things no one else wants to do and usually has to do with blood, bodily fluids or bulls, at least at our house." Dustin laughed and motioned toward the facilities. "Is everything ready for the big boy? Hopefully, you have the chicken wire up and stretched."

Seth was coming to understand that Dustin had a wicked sense of humor. It might perhaps be a bit warped at times but it was still a good one. "Don't worry. It's ready. I put up two layers of wire today. That should keep your baby under control until he chases me out of the pen."

Dustin studied Seth. "He hasn't made an effort to hurt us, which is part of the reason we thought he might work out for Travis. He is a sweetheart of a bull. So long as he doesn't get confused with one of the rodeo bulls around here for Zane, it all should be good."

Seth checked the area and couldn't think of anything else they needed to do before unloading. He turned to Dustin. "I think we're ready...*if* you can back that big rig up the little bitty walkway." He winked at Dustin.

Dustin cocked an eye for a few seconds before breaking a smile. "You want to make sure I don't run over anybody. I'll have this trailer kissing your gate in the blink of an eye."

Seth watched as Dustin maneuvered the trailer. He hadn't boasted about having the gift. Seth felt certain that the opening was only an inch of clearance on either side of his gooseneck trailer. Seth took the time to be certain that everything was the way Dustin wanted it, and it must have been, because before long, he was coming down from the truck, ready to open the gate.

"How's that?" Dustin asked.

"Everything as advertised."

Seth chuckled and began to open the gates leading into the pen. A few seconds later he was surprised at the heat of a warm muzzle against the back of his neck. Dustin had decided that letting the bull loose early to screw with him would be funny.

Seth slogged his way toward the fence and Jackson sniffed him the whole way. It was like being inspected by a giant dog. A few sniffs later and Seth ran for the fence, scrabbling as he hit the ground in front of a laughing Dustin.

"Are you crazy or just stupid?" Seth asked him, a little breathless.

"If I have to make a choice, I'd say I'm crazy. 'Stupid' has some implications I would just as soon avoid at this time." Dustin started to snicker.

Seth shook his head in disbelief, feeling lucky that the bull was an enormous pet. He took a deep breath, looked back and turned to Dustin. "Jackson seems to be settling in fine. Would you like to go inside? Maybe have something cold to drink?"

Dustin made a face that had Seth chuckling and explained, "I'm not a big fan of sweet tea. Yes, I realize it's the requirement to live in Texas. Yes, I know everyone else loves it. It does nothing for me."

Seth replied, "I hate sweet tea too. It makes me want to gag. But how do you feel about root beer?"

Dustin didn't miss a beat. "I *love* root beer. I like it more than just about anything, including real beer."

Seth headed for the house, tugging Dustin behind him. Once they were in the kitchen, Seth searched for bottles of root beer. He found the stash, popped the top off two of them and handed one to Dustin.

Dustin lifted a cold bottle and took a drink. Seth joined him, but before they stopped, they had each drained their bottles. Without a comment, Seth handed Dustin another before taking a second one for himself.

"That stuff is amazing. I've had nothing like that since I was a kid in Colorado. The old man who owned the store made his own homemade root beer. It was freaking delicious."

Seth hauled two more bottles of different flavors out and gave one to Dustin

"Try this one. Let me know what you think."

They went through the same routine with the new bottles, enjoying themselves thoroughly. Without warning, Dustin skipped topics and nodded toward Seth. "I know you from somewhere. Where?"

Seth shrugged his shoulders. "It could've been anywhere. My son's on the junior rodeo circuit. His name is Zane."

"It has to be because of him. I remember the name. The kid's a crazy-good bull rider. He made the rest of the youngsters look like amateurs."

"Yeah, that was us. He did one of your weeklong rodeo schools for bull riders. The classes were packed.

"How is he doing now? He was damn good at that age. He must be outstanding now."

Seth let out a sigh. "He's doing okay, still rough around the edges on some things. And sometimes it's more about grandstanding than it is about getting points."

Dustin nodded. "I have a class coming up, a bunch of eleven- and twelve-year-old kids. I could use someone experienced to help teach — or at least keep them out of trouble. I'd be willing to trade your son's help for some lessons during the week. What would you think of that arrangement?"

Seth started opening his mouth like a goldfish from one of the games at the state fair. *A weeklong private session?* That could help enough for Zane to win the finals *and* the scholarship he needed.

Seth tried to dial down his excitement and the new level of possibility for Zane. He focused on Dustin. "I'll talk with my son, but I don't see a reason not to take advantage of your offer."

Chapter Six

Travis paused for a moment, glancing back at Amy. They had volunteered to help Zane and Seth move the last of their stuff from their house in the suburbs to the ranch. Seth and Zane had initially moved in with just their necessities on the same day Travis had invited them, and they hadn't thought they'd need to bring over much more, but now that Travis and Seth were finalizing the merging of two families, they'd found that they could have used three times the space.

Now they were down to the last ten percent of the move that seemed to take ninety percent of the time. The only good thing to come out of all of it was that Seth already had an offer on his house, so his worries about money — at least for a while — would be put to rest. Travis decided that must be one benefit of living in the suburbs outside of a huge metroplex.

Travis stood for a moment, stretching his back as he surveyed the wall of boxes they had stuffed in Zane's room.

"Is that about it? It seems like we've moved a semi's-load of clothes and boy stuff into here," said Amy. "It could be worse, though. He could be a sports nut. Then we would've had all the crap from every kind of professional sports league. At least now it's only bull riding." She motioned to the pile of leather, wool and metal that dominated one corner. "Although I don't know what he's doing with fourteen cowbells. That seems excessive to me."

Travis shrugged then started shifting boxes again "I don't know, but I never rode bulls. Some of them are trophies and only a few are legitimate bull-rider bells.

After moving around the rest as best they could, Amy signaled their retreat. "I don't know what else to do with this crap. He's going to have to figure out where to store it. Maybe some in the barn?" she suggested to Travis, and he detected a hint of jealousy.

With that statement Amy seemed to lose her energy, because she walked to the corner of the bed, shoved the Zane equipment and memorabilia to one side, then collapsed. Travis thought it might be a good time to give her some news. "I'm getting an idea...maybe a way to help save the ranch."

Amy straightened herself and smiled. "Is this the infamous bull riding school that I've heard you and Seth talking about?" Amy asked.

Travis spared a glare at the spoiled surprise. "Maybe. There might be more to it than you realize."

"And what would that be? Gymnastics outfits for the barrel racers?"

"Well, I helped you pick out your outfits when you were running the barrels. But what I meant was that I will need more help planning. We're going to accept girls into any of the events they're interested in, so I'll need your perspective and advice on some of the issues that it will raise."

Travis smiled to himself when Amy stared at him open-mouthed.

"*Any* event? Even bull riding?" Amy asked.

"Yes, any of the events, including bull riding. Seth and I agree that anybody should be able to learn about any skill they are interested in."

* * * *

Travis rinsed out his toothbrush, set it in the holder then walked out of the bathroom. Seth was already in bed, the pillows stuffed behind him as he continued to read the book in his hands. Travis wrapped up what he needed to do before he got into bed. Most of it was automatic anymore, and he wasn't sure whether that was good or not. When he pulled back the cotton sheets, he realized Seth was wearing nothing but a pair of formfitting boxer-briefs with a pouch that held his goods on display.

Instead of letting the situation embarrass him, he studied the man who had been sleeping beside him for some time now. He acted on impulse, stopped then wrapped his hand around the back of Travis' neck and pull him in for a soft kiss. Whatever interest in the book Travis had was completely gone as Seth's attention visibly overwhelmed him. Travis' blank expression made Seth chuckle.

He took a few minutes to gather himself. "I was going to talk to you about the conversation I had with Amy today. She's good with the new ideas."

"And now, how about you...after being properly distracted?" Seth asked, grinning.

"Now? Yeah, I'll tell you how I am after that move. I would like to do naughty things. "

Seth moved closer to the man who he had been dreaming about all this time when a huge noise stopped him.

He had no doubt as to the cause. It was one of the infrequent game nights the high schoolers held and tonight's festivities were at their house. That eliminated the possibility of adult fun for Travis and Seth. Even though their bedroom was supposed to be their private space, the host parents would have the task of keeping snacks flowing and being the adult presence for the event. Most of their night would be filled with the two them running snacks back and forth to the competitors.

Travis tensed for a few seconds then collapsed against Seth. The two of them cuddled for a bit longer until there was another crash. Travis gave Seth a quick peck on the cheek, then stood and began pulling on clothing. As he tugged on socks, he gave Seth his sad smile. "We have no chance of getting anything done tonight except making sandwiches and keeping the bowls of chips filled… Sorry."

Then it was Seth's turn for a moment of regret. "It will happen. I don't know when and I don't know how, but it will. It will be perfect, and we will remember it the rest of our lives."

* * * *

Seth woke slowly to a room that was far too bright. On most mornings he'd wake pre-dawn, but now it looked more like twelve-dark-thirty. The light was too much to go back to sleep. He struggled with waking up until he realized Travis was not in bed with him. He recalled the night before and thought they had played the respectable adults pretty well—although he would've rather played a raunchy college student.

He sat up in the bed and sniffed. Travis must be responsible for the black brew Seth had inhaled and needed. Seth had done his part of the job to feed the nocturnal eating monsters who had occupied them the previous night. As he struggled to wake up, he caught more of the aroma of strong black coffee, so he pulled on a T-shirt and jeans then headed downstairs.

Travis motioned him toward the table. "Seth, please join me. We can grab a few quiet minutes for a change." He gave him a glance and held up the coffee mug he'd been working on. "Grab a cup from the kitchen. I did a decent job on the morning-after coffee."

Seth nodded in acknowledgment and made his way to the huge pot of coffee sitting on the counter. He took one of the large mugs and poured himself enough to do the job of fully waking him. As he was stirring in the extras he preferred in his coffee, he realized that the counter was filled with more than just the magical drink. There was a sheet pan filled with an assortment of breads, donuts and pastries, along with butter, honey and several types of jelly.

Now Seth's biggest problem became deciding which treats he wanted to combine. A few minutes later he had fixed himself a mixture of sugar-laden delights that looked like something Zane might have concocted. Balancing the brimming plate, he made his way to the table where Travis was working on the last of his coffee, his breakfast and the comics.

As Travis folded the paper and set it to the side, Seth sat with him, then there was a snore so loud that it seemed like it could have come from seismic activity.

As the noise rippled away, it left Seth snickering." I can almost guarantee that was Zane. That boy snores like a buzz saw.

Seth took another sip of his coffee and looked around. "I don't hear any other close contenders. Sometimes kids feed the noise to each other. Adolescence seems to do weird things, especially to young boys. But I do sleep a lot better when there isn't a cluster of teenagers snoring enough to shake the walls."

"Hell, I have no idea when the last time was that we had a royal roof-raising. Those kinds of things tend to make a lasting impression on me."

Seth finished his fight with one of the better scones then leaned back in his chair, closing his eyes and feeling happy and content.

Travis stacked his plate silverware and Seth put his empty coffee mug beside it, which indicated that their leisurely morning had ended. "I'm going to pick up some things at Mesquite. I'll be gone for a couple of hours." He motioned to the immovable islands that were the various kids crashed around for the night. "The kids will clean up after themselves for the most part. You might have to remind them a few times that yes, they have to tidy up the mess afterward or there'll be no more parties — at least not anytime soon."

While Travis and Seth were visiting, Zane got up, stretched and joined them. "It will be spotless. Amy and I will make sure of it."

Seth watched as Travis made his way out to one of the barns, and before he could say anything, Zane turned to him with an interesting expression on his face. "We need to talk."

Seth cringed to hear those words. "Okay, what's up?"

"I think yesterday Amy and I were cock-blockers on you."

His face heated like a summer grass fire. He turned toward Zane but couldn't meet his gaze. "What do you mean? How could you be a cock-blocker to me?"

"Really? You're going to make me draw pictures? Okay, I think you and Travis were about to do the wild thing—if you hadn't already—when we descended on you."

Seth turned even redder. "Zane, I was going to tell you. It was just—"

"No, I'm not trying to bust you. I actually wanted to tell you I think Travis is cool and I like him a lot."

"Really?" Seth said.

"Sure. I think congrats are in order. Mom has been gone quite a while now and you've been alone too long. Besides, you know she wanted you to find someone else."

"But, Amy?"

Zane laughed. "I'm not going to out you. I'm also not telling Amy." Then there was an abrupt change in subject. "I'm not spending my day cleaning either. Let's get these shits awake."

Seth followed his son as Zane started waking the people around him in preparation to get the house back to the spotless condition he'd kept it.

* * * *

Seth walked out of the small cabin on Shane and Dustin's ranch into what felt like humid conditions—but he wouldn't complain. This was the weather in northern Texas in August. He sat on the front steps for a minute, thinking about what a great opportunity Dustin had given them to trade some private lessons for Zane's helping him wrangle his bull-riding class. He'd begun helping Zane, and even though they hadn't been there very long, he'd found several things Zane needed to work on.

Seth stayed still as the screen door creaked open then slammed shut. The sound of bare feet across well-worn wood let him know who it was. Zane was up for the day too.

"Morning, Zane. Dustin said last night that breakfast would be ready around seven." He studied his son and grinned with more than a little humor at his seeming disbelief. "That was kind of my reaction, but Dustin said they have breakfast after they've finished the first round of chores, which include feeding the pasture full of potential bulls ready to be inspected by a rodeo contractor out of Fort Worth."

Zane leaned against Seth in a familiar position for the two of them, more like the action of a ten-year-old than an eighteen-year-old. But Seth wouldn't question the closeness. They sat for a few minutes, Seth feeling the morning heat rising with each passing second. He heard somebody at the main house banging on the triangle.

"Breakfast's ready! Everyone who's eating better haul their ass to the table."

Seth chuckled, stood beside his son and extended a hand. "Come on. If we don't get down there, everything will be gone. With this bunch, not even the bad stuff will be left."

Zane took the offered hand, lifted himself upright then followed his father to the dining pavilion where a buffet was set up along one side and the rest of the space was littered with tables and chairs.

Dustin greeted them with a grin. "Morning, sleepyheads. Zane, I thought you'd be here before daylight to see what bulls the contractors were inspecting. We've got a couple that would challenge even an old-timer like me." Dustin chuckled.

Zane stood for a moment, making the strange lonely sound he did when he wasn't awake, then he attempted to tease Dustin. "I can talk the boss into showing me what stock contractors want. One might have my scholarship tattooed on his butt."

"You never know. Stranger things have happened. There was a bull named Diablo that kept me from winning the national finals one year. He was more than I could handle."

Shane had walked up behind them while they were chatting. He lifted his arm, wrapped it around Dustin's shoulders and gave him an affectionate squeeze. "People underestimated that bull. But things worked out for the best."

Dustin lifted from his melancholy. "That's right. Perseverance is important in this life. Even if we never won nationals, we have a reputation for rodeo stock that's lasted long past those days when I was competing."

He turned to Seth. "This is perfect for us. It might not be what everyone would want. There've been things we've tried that were complete failures. Some might work better for Travis than they did for us. Try things. Get your feet wet. Stretch those creative muscles."

Shane laughed and squeezed Dustin's shoulder. "I think they get the idea. You and your metaphors... For those of us who interpret the combinations you put together then try to explain them to someone else... Well, it's mind-blowing.

Dustin just smiled. "I don't need to be the champion. I do enjoy being in charge, though."

Shane rubbed his hand down Dustin's back. "I'm happy with you. That's the only thing that matters." He considered them all for a moment then shook his head. "Let's get going. We renovated one of our barns. It was either fix it up or burn it down. Now that it's all renovated, it even has unisex bathrooms. But this first batch is all boys, six of them. That will make it easier to work out how to handle them."

"Well, I'll work on getting the bull ready and give him a morning treat," said Dustin. "Finish your breakfast and come find me when you're done." He nodded his head toward Seth. "I've got some ideas for how you two could expand on the idea of the rodeo school. And, Seth, you seem to have kept Zane at a good pace. Let's see what you think of the arrangements I worked out for these boys."

The energy of the room dropped when Dustin left. Seth wasn't sure whether the guy was a positive force or a drain. But either way, he really liked the guy.

Shane followed Seth's stare as Dustin made it to the next task he'd given himself. "He's always like that...a ball of energy. It's a lot easier to go along with him than resist."

Seth strained to decide if a reply was needed when Zane tugged at his sleeve.

"Dad, I don't want to be late for the first event on Dustin's list."

Seth started then realized he was being chastised and fell into the buffet line with his son.

After their meal, Zane spent the next hour with Dustin at the bull riding classes. Seth watched the youngsters trying to hold on for those precious eight seconds and gathered ideas that might help Travis in his plans for a similar school. Things were going well, and more important, Dustin seemed happy with the progress Zane was making. There had been a couple of encounters early on as the two headstrong alpha males had butted heads. But by the end of the first morning Dustin had established himself.

From there on out, Zane's only replies were 'yes, sir' and 'no, sir'.

As the hours and days progressed, Seth was more and more pleased with the way Dustin handled the youngsters. They'd ended up with five of the prepubescent monsters because one didn't make it through the initial day before he'd headed back home. But the other students were serious about what they were doing. Dustin was keeping them busy and got the respect he deserved. He was a more civilized than Zane, and their relationship had become a type of hero-worship.

They'd intended for Zane to be the nighttime caretaker for the campers. Instead, he had been responsible for many of their more outlandish stunts. But, by and large, everybody did what they were supposed to do as individuals, and later, when they were working together. The final activity was a bull-riding competition. The boys were eager to show the skills they'd learned, and the mentors could let their teaching abilities shine.

The first buzzer sounded and the full volume of the rider's cowbell clattering like a crazed holiday choir left no doubt as to the pending success of the event. The countdown started, and everyone held their breath for the eight seconds the young man needed to stay on board. Time passed with the speed of molasses on a cold winter's night, and the bull was jumping like he was riding a pogo stick.

The buzzer sounded and Seth bought himself a breath of air. First bull rider—no injuries, no tears, no upset parents. Those were all good things, so far as Seth was concerned. A few adjustments might be needed for the next session, but everything was running as much like a real rodeo as possible.

Before Seth realized what was happening, the next bull was in his chute. He saw a bit more panic in this one's eyes. But the kids had ridden each bull a multitude of times, so Seth knew this boy would perform to the best of his ability. The rider was in the school on the scholarship awarded from Dustin and Shane. He was competitive on a level beyond his classmates but his single mother couldn't afford the fees for him to participate.

With no excuses, she'd emailed, explaining why her child wanted to be in the rodeo. Seth had told her there was financial help for those who needed it. The email hadn't been asking for special dispensation, rather to determine their options, an explanation from one parent to another—which had been the point of giving the scholarship. Seth had been glad the teen had taken his opportunity.

The tension passed, and before Seth knew what was happening, the kid had nodded his head. What followed was both wonderful and heart-pounding. The performance made all of them proud. The seconds ticked by until the buzzer sounded. In the stands it sounded like the people had come unhinged.

The rodeo ticked off the participants with each of them performing at their best. Once it was over, the contestants and their parents said their goodbyes. Eventually, the ranch returned to normal and even Dustin and Shane seemed thankful. But when they had all retreated to the porch with frosty glasses of lemonade and completed their postmortem on the week, Shane announced, "We're sure glad you all came, and now we have a surprise for Zane."

The young man twisted to catch the expression on everyone's faces. Seth did nothing more than ready himself for any possibility.

"Well, day after tomorrow night is the state qualifier in junior division. It's here in Wichita Falls. We cleaned the arena and picked out a few of the bulls that would likely be high scoring. We thought you might like to stay a couple more days. We can do some practice rides here so you can work more on what you've learned over the last week. It could be a great way to hone those new skills then put them to the test."

Zane swallowed hard then shot him a smile "I think that would be perfect. Then I can show the others how it's done."

* * * *

Two days and several practice rounds later, Seth sat in the arena bleachers, watching the competition.

One thing he knew. Some of these bulls were as nasty as any he'd seen on the adult circuit. Zane's run was coming soon, and he didn't want to miss the ride.

"The kids have to make sure they stayed focused. At this point in the competition, a rider can easily become injured," said Dustin as he joined him in the grandstands.

Seth replied, "That is why I'm sitting here white-knuckling it. Otherwise I'd be 'that' parent."

Dustin started to say something else but when they saw that Zane was on his bull, both of them fell silent. Seth could name off the items from Zane's mental checklist. In a few seconds, Seth heard nothing more than the soft rattle of Zane's cowbell.

He pushed his helmet on tight and signaled the gateman with a quick flip of his head. As the chute swung open, everything moved into slow motion for Seth.

The bull curled into a ball then exploded out with a power Seth hadn't often seen. He spun, jumped and bucked his way across the dusty arena.

A few seconds into the round Zane's goal visibly shifted from winning the competition to surviving the ride.

"What a trip," Dustin said. "I'm damn glad Shane is one of the bull fighters."

Seth had forgotten Dustin was still beside him. It eased his concern that Shane was a bull fighter...but only slightly. The final time flashed then the eight-second timer sounded.

The ride's over. All we need to do now is get him off the bull and out of the arena.

He could tell Zane was waiting for an opportunity. An instant later he tensed then jumped. Seth saw what he was doing and could have exploded with frustration. He was trying for a signature dismount. Him being able to walk through the gate would have been enough to satisfy his parent. But Zane had begun, and Seth could do nothing but wait...and pray.

Zane spun like a trick rider, waved to the crowd then did a flip off the animal.

He landed. Everything's good.

Zane began to back out of the arena, waving. But the bull decided he hadn't finished and started a run at Zane. He'd just stepped back when disaster struck. Seth watched in horror when Zane sprawled across the floor after a two-thousand-pound bull flipped him like a ragdoll.

Almost before he realized what he was doing, he was kneeling beside Zane. Terrified by the extent of his injuries, he cradled Zane's right hand. He realized the EMT was talking with him.

"He got off lucky. A banged-up hand and maybe a few cracked ribs. It could have been worse."

The world spun for Seth as he tried to take in everything. Then he mimicked the EMT like a parrot. "Could have been worse…"

* * * *

Seth woke in the dim light of the bedroom he shared with Travis. The past week had been a mishmash of disasters with the potential to shut down the careful plans he and Zane had been creating for years. To their good fortune, the triage in the arena had been incorrect. The ribs were bruised but nothing was worse. Zane was just finding that trying to take deep breaths was a new challenge.

But he did have broken bones in his right hand, the one he needed to ride with. Their doctor had confirmed the X-ray. The hand had taken serious abuse. Those bones couldn't hold up to being stepped on by a bull. So, the Davis team was sidelined for the next six weeks.

Seth became more coherent, realizing he wasn't the only one awake. As he snuggled his back against Travis, he discovered something else. Travis was sporting his morning erection. It wasn't like this was a new occurrence, but it was the first time Travis hadn't just slipped to the bathroom to relieve himself. This time Seth was ready. He wanted to have a relationship with this man beyond friendship, but he didn't want to put Travis in an unwelcomed situation.

Seth squeaked when a muscular arm encircled his chest. Travis tugged Seth closer and pressed against him. With another thrust of his hips, Travis wedged his erection between the cloth-covered globes of Seth's ass.

"Where are you headed with that thing?" Seth asked.

"Where would you like for it to go? I'm tired of jacking off in the shower."

Travis pushed his hand lower, letting his fingernails slide over Seth's flat stomach. Another few seconds of that left Seth hard and ready for action. He smiled at Travis. "I think I'm ready to move to the next step, and someone else gets to just be buddies."

Seth luxuriated in the attention he was getting from Travis. The texture of Travis' chest against his back sent pulses of desire rolling through Seth. A thought came to him that he would have preferred to ignore, but he couldn't bring himself to do so.

"We can't do this...not with the kids in the house." Seth sighed and started to scoot away from Travis.

Travis tightened his hold on Seth, curling around his body just as Seth had always hoped he would. "Remember... The kids are gone for sleepovers or something and won't recover until this afternoon. That gives us several hours for exploring."

A crackle of pleasure rippled through Seth's body. He'd forgotten that the kids were gone. He'd wanted to have Travis writhing like a horny teenager, and it'd been so long since he had been intimate with anybody, either.

"Travis, all this feels great. Remember, though, that you have so much at stake with Amy. Life is a lot less subtle from my angle, raising a son. Do you want to risk what you have now?"

Travis began, "I'm tired of doing what's safe and ready to enjoy our time together. Amy will deal with it. Maybe it might be a little tough at first, but I'm sure she'll adjust."

Travis nibbled Seth's shoulder, sending desire spiraling through his body again. What little intimacy they'd shared already had left Seth with a wet spot across the front of his underwear. Travis leaned close and, at the last second, Seth turned his head so their lips met. They froze for a moment, each clearly relishing the exchange. Seth broke the kiss, rolled over to face Travis then lifted his hands to either side of Travis' face, cupping his cheeks gently.

"You are an amazing guy, Travis. Please let me know what you want to do and how far we're going to go."

Seth tightened his hold on Travis, pulling them together until they shared a deep kiss. Time slipped past, the passion growing beyond Seth's bearing with each touch. The morning breeze rustled the curtains in the bedroom, giving a kiss of the outside to their growing fervor. Several long minutes passed, and Seth was becoming more and more urgent in his desire to be with Travis much closer, much more intimately.

Travis twisted and Seth found himself covered by a man who was obviously equally in need of relief. Soon they were grinding against each other, Seth's lust was heightened further, though he didn't think that was possible.

Travis ran his hands over Seth's body several times, teasing his erect nipples with each pass. Because they were one of his favorite erogenous zones, Seth did all he could to encourage Travis.

"That's it. Travis, you are *so* sexy. What do you want to do next?" asked Seth.

Travis chuckled and ground his rock-hard cock against Seth. "I think we should ditch the underwear and get down to some serious business."

Seth groaned, shoving his pelvis to grind against Travis again. "That sounds like an excellent idea. I was hoping to slap your naked butt, cowboy."

Travis scrambled off the bed, pushed his underwear to his ankles then stepped out of them. With his backside still facing Seth, he did a dance that set his butt to wiggling. "Is this the ass you want to slap? You want a piece of this?"

"Nice, very nice. I knew those Wranglers showed off your best advantage, and the answer to both questions is not just 'yes' but a 'hell, yes'."

"So, my backside is the stuff of wet dreams. Look what happens in front," Travis said.

Travis turned and Seth licked his lips, studying Travis' thick cock, which was so hard it was aimed to the sky, and toying with his own pre-cum-covered cockhead through his briefs.

Travis shook his turgid cock at Seth and smiled. "All right, big guy. You ready to see what I've got for you?

From what I can tell so far, Christmas has just come early for both of us."

Grinning from ear to ear, Seth crawled across the bed, slipped off the side and stopped a few feet from Travis.

He spread his legs, cupping his package with one hand while running his other hand over his chest. He ran the tip of his tongue along his upper lip as he shot Travis a hungry glance, teasing him. He reached lower, squeezing his ball sac. Travis was breathing harder. With that, Seth slipped his fingers in the elastic on each side of his briefs and worked them down his hips. More and more of his bush became exposed until the root of his cock was visible above it. In a smooth motion, Seth pull the underwear down his thighs then let them drop to the floor.

He squeezed the base of his dick, gave it a pull and smirked at Travis. "So, what do you think?"

Seth didn't wait for an answer, though. He stepped closer, running his hands over Travis' butt and letting a few fingers trail between his muscular ass cheeks. He pressed their bodies together, rubbing against him and coating the two of them with pre-cum. Then Seth reached between them, swiped a finger through the clear fluid from the tip of Travis' cock and slipped it into his mouth. He nearly groaned at the hungry gaze Travis had locked on him.

Travis drew a deep breath then finally said, "I think you're hot, unbelievably intense. All I want to do is make love with you this morning then see where it goes from there. But right now I'm gonna combust if you don't touch me...and soon."

Seth moaned at that declaration and wrapped one of his hands around their combined cocks. Travis' granite-hard shaft felt delightful in his grip. The pre-cum covered both their dicks, making everything slick. Seth closed his teeth over one of Travis' nipples, tugging it before flicking his tongue against its erect tip. The result must have flashed through Travis like a wildfire because his body shook as Seth moved to the other side and repeated his action. Each time Seth worked his nipples, Travis' moans became louder. Soon Seth was holding him and they were kissing deeply as they ground their bodies together and Seth worked their joined cocks.

Then Seth released his grasp to a pained groan by Travis, took him by the hand and guided him back to the bed. Travis eased himself onto the mattress, moving away from the edge.

"Come on, Seth. This is the hottest time I've had in years. I plan on enjoying it until we both explode."

Seth took in the view in front of him, considering it a work of natural beauty. Travis had the perfect amount of dark swirls across his chest that plunged down the trail to form a thick thatch around his uncut shaft. He reached down to stroke himself as he watched Travis. He'd enjoyed their teasing so far, but Seth didn't know how much longer he could hold out.

He had awakened horny, and now he was far beyond simply that. With a final hard squeeze to his own dick, Seth crawled into the bed beside Travis, leaned down and kissed his throat. Seth enjoyed the texture of stubble on Travis' face. He was without a doubt as hot a man as Seth had ever been with.

"Good," said Seth." I don't think I can last much longer."

"Yeah, me too. I'm so hard I could cut diamonds."

Seth gave him a smile that he hoped said it all, then began taking Travis like an animal in heat. He pushed forward until he pinned Travis against the mattress then he rested his hands on either side of Travis' head and lowered himself until the entire length of their naked bodies were intertwined.

Seth lifted back, gasping for air, then he rolled to the side, leaned down and wrapped his hand around Travis' dick. The pre-cum was leaking from its tip like a running garden hose. He paused, holding the shaft a few inches away from his lips as he studied Travis. Travis' expression assured Seth that he was ready, more than ready, for the next step.

Seth slipped his lips around Travis' cock, forcing a loud moan from the cowboy. This time the buildup was more rapid. He took the first few inches down his throat and was overwhelmed by the taste and scent of the man. He'd forgotten what it was like to have sex with another man, the musky, earthy tastes and smells, especially a man he found so attractive.

Seth pumped his mouth up and down around Travis' cock, deeper with each pass until it reached the back of his throat. He swallowed and pressed his lips against Travis' crotch.

"Oh my God! That's it. It feels so fucking good," moaned Travis.

Seth wanted Travis' experience to be one he would never forget. He slipped his fingers lower, teasing between his legs and stroking across his balls.

"Oh God, you've got to stop. I'll explode if you don't," Travis pleaded.

Seth pulled off until he was flicking his tongue over the tip of Travis' cock before he slipped off and twisted around to give him a passionate kiss. Then he collapsed, lying against the bed as the erotic sensation washed over him. Seth slid his fingers over Travis' hair and smiled. "Need a bit of an intermission?"

"Give me a second. We were close to being finished — or at least I was."

Then Travis turned the tables and began to work. Sensations rippled through Seth from the tips of his ears to his curled toes when Travis took his cock and swallowed it to the root. He trembled as Travis began to pump up and down, coating his shaft with saliva that mixed with copious amounts of his pre-cum.

The oh-so-familiar sensation of orgasm began to work its way through Seth's body. The ecstasy drew him closer and closer to the edge, nearing his finale. Seth was on the brink and his muscles contracted as his balls drew tight against his dick. He tried to squirm away, but Travis had him under his control. He spread his legs wider, his toes curling from the delicious sensations.

"Travis. Dude. I'm almost…"

Travis slipped his head down Seth's cock then paused for a second and eased back up, not appearing to care. A short time later, Seth was bucking like a wild animal, losing all sensation beyond his need for release.

Every muscle in his body locked. Travis writhed himself free and began to stroke him. The need for release curled over Seth, his cock throbbing with pleasure. He erupted, the first thick white strand leaving a trail over his chest almost to his belly button. Lucid thought ended for several amazing minutes. He was delirious as lines and pools of white covered his torso while Travis worked every drop from him. The aching sweet response slipped by until Seth shot his final volley and melted into the bed.

"Oh. My. God. I think my brain has turned into mush." He lifted himself and winked at Travis. "If you were trying to prove something, you definitely have. I haven't felt this spacey since college. But we aren't finished here…"

Travis was waiting with a grin — and a very stiff-looking cock bobbing against his abdomen.

Seth raced into their bathroom, grabbed a thick towel and wiped himself clean then tossed it onto the counter. He stalked back across the room, moved between Travis' legs and spread them wide. Then he began a furious attack of tongue, fingers and lips to give Travis at least a comparable experience to the one he'd just had. The soft sounds of sex filled the space, accompanied with the fresh, heady sounds of Travis' moans of pleasure.

Seth was exploring Travis' cock, sucking and licking it from the tip to the base. The cowboy was getting closer, his body indicating he was nearly ready for release.

"Not much more… I'm *so* close," Travis muttered.

Then Seth dug the tip of his tongue into Travis' cock slit.

"Oh, fuck!" Travis called out.

Seth swallowed what Travis gave, knowing his release would go on for a while. But Seth enjoyed each spend. With a final muscle convulsion, Seth's mouth was filled with Travis' essence. A split second later, Travis collapsed on the bed, gasping for air.

When they calmed, Seth went to the bathroom for a wet rag and the towel and cleaned both of them. Then they curled against each other, enjoying the scent of mind-blowing sex that had filled the room. Seth gave Travis a light kiss, then whispered, "That was amazing.

It was the first time since... Well, you don't have to worry about anything. I'm clean."

Travis grinned in return. "Me too, clean as a whistle. No sex and an annual check. You can't get safer than us." He dragged Seth over him like a woolen comforter and sighed.

"Let's catch some more sleep. Hot sex always makes me want to nap."

Seth wrapped himself around Travis and kissed his cheek. "Sounds like a great idea. I'm exhausted."

But it seemed like almost instantly Seth was awakened by the sound of voices and the rattling of the porch door. He lunged in panic, untangled himself from Travis and their bedding then shook Travis, hard.

"Get up! The kids are home."

Travis woke in a quick series of bounds. And a few seconds later they were in various states of dress when they heard, "Dad? Are you here?"

Chapter Seven

Travis' frustration bubbled over and he flung the pencil across the room. It skated along the far wall, giving him a moment of satisfaction. Then he realized there had been a witness to his stunt. He intertwined his fingers behind his head, leaned back in his chair and turned to Seth.

"So, how long have you been standing there watching me make an ass of myself?"

"I missed most of the performance. I was just here for the grand finale of the pencil flying across the room. Do you need to do the other part?" Seth asked.

"And what would that entail?" Travis said.

Seth's comment accompanied a juvenile snicker. "Well, it's the whole crumble up the paper and throw it. Or if you're going for the maximum effect, you sweep everything off your desk onto the floor. That's when things are really strong." Seth walked close, took Travis' shoulders in his hands and started massaging them. "So, now that you've had your explosion, what can I do?"

Travis chuckled. "Do you have several thousand dollars doing nothing? That might help out things. But since you're unemployed and I'm running a failing ranch, I don't see where that money is coming from. This would be one of those classic times you have to have money to make money. I guess I could sell off the yearlings." He turned to Seth. "But that defeats the purpose, wouldn't you say?"

Seth found a tense muscle in Travis' neck and focused on it for the next few seconds.

Travis went on. "Dustin and Shane are coming this morning to tour our facilities. Maybe they can give me suggestions for the rodeo school idea."

"So, be the turtle," Seth said.

"Turtle?"

"Yeah, like a big, old turtle. Things get rough and you have your own built-in armor."

"Well, a bit of a turtle. We're still working out details on how things might come together." Travis started putting his desk and the room back in order. "You know how Shane and Dustin are. I don't want them with us in the middle of more drama."

It was just a few minutes later when Travis heard Shane's diesel dually pickup pulling into the driveway. The roar left no question as to who was arriving. At least he and Seth would be in a circle of friends.

Travis stepped out with Seth just behind him and returned Dustin's enthusiastic wave as they came to a stop. Travis let the two men exit their truck and get closer to the house before he stepped off the front porch and met them in the middle of the yard.

He grabbed Dustin's hand in a tight grip, glad to see their friends again. The cowboy returned the handshake with equal enthusiasm. "Hey, glad to see you guys made it. Hopefully, you didn't run into any bad weather or drunk truck drivers on your way here."

Shane chuckled for a second as he took Travis' hand and pumped it in greeting. "No, nothing dramatic like that, just the normal — taking a stock trailer on Loop 20 around Fort Worth."

Travis released Shane and chuckled at the comment. "I hear you. I've told Seth many times that they should make that one of the new attractions at Six Flags Over Texas. It would be a ride nobody would ever forget."

Dustin snorted. "Or live through. But hey, we're all busy men. Let's see what you got. Maybe there's something we can do to help you with your plans."

Travis nodded. "Dustin is right. I've wasted enough time today, pushing numbers around that didn't want to be cooperative. But it will all be good when you help us discover what we need. Zane has been practicing in the arena, so it won't take much to put that in order and the same thing with the barrel racing and pole bending facilities. Amy's been using them," Travis said.

On an impulse, Travis leaned into Seth and kissed him. "You're welcome to come along, but I know you wanted to finish something."

"I can come up with lunch. There are some leftovers from last night," Seth said.

Travis smiled his thanks then motioned for Shane and Dustin to follow him. He was anxious as to how they would react to him using the ranch as a school. Travis led them to the door, ready to see what possibilities existed that he and Seth had not already identified.

It took longer for the tour than Travis had anticipated. Shane and Dustin had a lot more questions than he'd expected. All of them made sense when

Travis considered them, but a high percentage didn't tie into setting up the school.

The other topics the men had queried were side events they could do to help them raise funds, like food trucks to give the parents something to enjoy and link in the grass-fed beef they were marketing. Then there were the more technical issues, like how to divide up kids who might range in age from a nine-year-old girl to eighteen-year-old boys and keep it fair and safe. But as they worked through the problems, Travis became more encouraged. They were close to having what they needed. It would just be a matter of funding.

Travis told Shane and Dustin to wait on the porch while he went to check on Seth, who was finishing his preparations on lunch. He glanced up when Travis came in and grabbed a few drinks from the fridge. Travis paused for a moment and shot Seth a grin. "The time is whizzing by," Travis said. "What delicious grub are you making us for lunch?"

Seth spun up a damp towel and snapped Travis' ass. Travis squeaked and dove for the door.

As he made his hasty exit, Seth called, "Serves you right, you tease. I'll let you know when it's ready."

Travis joined Shane and Dustin, and they went over a bunch of tiny details they hadn't tackled earlier. They had made sizable in-roads into the list when a clanging racket filled the air. Travis chuckled and rose, motioning for the others to follow him.

"That would be Seth on the triangle announcing that if we want hot food, we had better get our butts in gear."

About the time Travis started to make another comment, Dustin's stomach growled in an impressive imitation of a lion. He gave Travis a guilt-free smirk.

"Time to eat. After my stomach makes sounds like that, I'm not good for anything until I have food in me anyway."

With the shake of his head, Travis beckoned them into the house. "Since we would consider you guys company, I'm sure Seth has the back porch set up. He's been waiting for a day when it's cool enough to use. Today will work."

The three of them made their way around to the large screened-in porch Travis had installed two years earlier. It had all the necessary kitchen equipment, including an outdoor stove and refrigerator. Interestingly enough, Shane had decided it would be a great addition to the rodeo school. Gourmet food at its finest. He thought they might even bring in chefs from the metroplex and give cooking lessons.

When they walked in, Travis was a little taken aback by what Seth had set up. The layout was more than he'd expected. Seth even had quart mason jars filled with something to drink. Travis gave it a sniff then cocked his head and smiled at Seth. "That's lemonade, not sweet tea. What are you trying to pull?"

"No, there's sweet tea for you. It's for those of us who don't like iced tea, like me, Shane and Dustin. Although I hear that if you put enough sugar in it, it's drinkable."

Travis glanced from Seth to the other before shrugging his shoulders. "I guess that's your way of telling me you want something they enjoy — and that's good. But sweet tea works just fine for me."

Seth put the last of the meal on the table and sat beside Travis.

"Everyone dig in. I've fixed enough to feed a small army. If you leave hungry, you have no one to blame for it but yourself." He reached up and took a few pieces of bread, spun the lazy Susan and started making a sandwich that Dagwood of cartoon fame would appreciate.

It didn't take long for the rotating platter to become decimated and the men relaxed. Seth popped the last bite into his mouth and gestured to the group. "So, how are things going? What was the prognosis on turning the ranch into a rodeo school?"

Shane and Dustin looked at each other before Dustin turned back to Seth and said, "The bull riding you nailed. Just add a few more animals so there is a good rotation in your program. The pole bending and barrel racing? There's not much more you have to do there either. A little touching up on a few things and you're ready for the students to start. You may find more trouble getting teachers for those events, though. It's outside of our bailiwick."

Seth listened intently.

"I don't know how Dustin feels, but I'm glad that you're not gonna be competition for us, because you can do more. Plus, you can pull from the metroplex for students and teachers since you aren't that far away. You're close to one of the major rodeo markets. Your potential is good enough that I offered to teach a couple of weeklong sessions on bullfighting."

Travis nodded in agreement, a big grin lighting up his face. "Kind of took me by surprise, but it makes sense. Some kids would want to get into bullfighting too. It's a different toolset but it could still be fun and just another way that we can expand our offerings. Besides, I need somebody to help pull those crazy bull riders out of the arena."

Seth nodded, considered for a few moments then went ahead with his question. "What about the mixed gender rule? Is that policy a good one, a bad idea or just what we have to do because it's the right thing?"

This time Dustin jumped into the conversation before anyone else could speak. "It's something you *have* to do. It might also be something that *should* be done, though it sometimes becomes a task that has the same number of minuses as pluses. But we all agreed that we are examples. We have to at least do our best to update rodeo, even if it's only for our ten-student school."

Seth nodded as he gave Dustin a serious glance. "Those were our thoughts too. If nothing else, it is time for change. Rodeo needs to realize the potential for girls to be bull riders and the boys to ride the barrels — or any other combination of participation a kid is interested in."

Seth started clearing the table as he talked. "There are a lot of ideas in the works. When will it all begin to happen?"

Travis chuckled. "We'll have that conversation once we find a way to fund all the pieces. Don't forget that our opening facilities are minimal, and none of us know anything about buying the horses or who might teach bronc riding. So, there are still details to work out."

Dustin slapped Shane on the knee. "Right, babe. We are not anywhere near being finished on the details of their school today." He turned to Travis and Seth. "You've got a hell of a start, though. Anything we can do to help, let us know. Because of how far we are from each other, we don't see you as competition but a part of a network of people trying to figure out how to make a living in modern-day agriculture and try to make some headway in making rodeo more attainable to any younger who is interested. Working couples help keep conversations interesting."

Once they had wrapped up the plans for the next steps, Shane and Seth decided to go over the breeding records to see what kind of bulls they might have coming up. Dustin and Travis made their way to the barn. After a little bit, Dustin stopped outside one of the pens and watched the cattle. Travis stepped up to enjoy the quiet with him but Dustin surprised him when he spoke up.

"Are you guys having problems?" Dustin asked.

Travis was jolted into the realization that Dustin was more perceptive than he thought. He took a few seconds to gather his thoughts, but once he had, he answered truthfully. "Only the financial challenges. That said, years ago, when our kids started doing the Junior Rodeo circuit, we made an agreement that we were off limits for each other, that we were better off staying friends."

Dustin shot him a cockeyed grin. "Things have changed now?"

"Just a little, wouldn't you say? We're living together."

"How's that working out for you?"

Travis shot him a grin. "Tense, very tense. There isn't much personal time at a house with two teenagers. We've had a few near misses."

"Fuck, that's why we don't have any kids. Shane's nieces and nephews are enough. I have to get laid on a regular basis or I get bitchy." Dustin grinned as he studied Travis then started again. "I'll talk to Shane and see if he has any ideas. He's a pretty sharp cookie sometimes."

"Any suggestions for now?"

Dustin snorted. "Sex toys. I have a collection of dildos."

The heat washed over Travis' face as he took off toward Seth. Just that idea made him want to get his hands on his lover as soon as possible, and though a kiss would have to do for now, it was better than nothing.

Dustin shouted, "And they aren't all mine."

* * * *

Seth walked through the house in full comfort mode. He was barefoot and wearing gym shorts with a loose T-shirt that had seen better days, but he was comfortable as hell.

He reached his desk and spread out the paperwork he needed to deal with that day. All the bookkeeping for the ranch had become his domain, and he was okay with that. He had started untangling the mess Travis' paperwork had been, from expense sheets to registration forms to sales. Someone had shoved them in a boot box, probably in the hope that they would either organize themselves or melt away. He hated to tell Travis, but nothing was going to disappear.

Seth lost himself in the task, enjoying untangling the puzzles the ranch supplied. He had been at it for at least half the morning when he realized he needed a snack and something to drink. As he rifled through the fridge, he grabbed a bottle of Hill Country root beer. As he remembered the delicious flavor, and the positive experience with the father-son pair, he snapped off the cap and made his way back to his work.

He had become focused on the numbers again when a sharp rap came from the porch. *What the hell? No one should be coming by today. The kids are at some action movie and Travis took a trip to the East Texas piney woods.* He set his work aside and started making his way to the door.

He peered through the window and the sight shocked him. Hank stood on his porch, and with him was another man who Seth could only describe as hotter than fuck. He remembered how he was dressed. His first inclination was to stall, sprint to the bedroom and change into business clothes, but after a moment he discovered he'd picked up more of Travis' easy-going attitude than he'd realized and opened the door. He'd concluded that they'd hunted him down and chosen to arrive on his doorstep unplanned, not the other way around.

To the pair's credit, they had no reaction when he opened the door. Seth was anxious to see what reason they gave for their appearance at Travis' home. He'd love to hear the story of how they found the ranch at all but that could wait. First things first.

"Hi, Hank. I haven't seen you in — well, since Craig closed the firm and dumped all of his employees."

The model-handsome man cocked an eyebrow at Hank. "I told you it was a bad idea to not talk to him sooner. No one likes to be left twisting in the wind. I wouldn't blame Seth if he told us to hit the road." At surface value, the stranger's statement seemed to put Seth in the catbird seat, but he was more than aware that the firm's closing left him with more like pigeon-shit.

Seth started to voice a reply when Hank cut him off. "Sorry about that, Seth. TJ is right. Not contacting you sooner was a stupid stunt. I hope you will still consider working with us."

Before Seth could get past the shocking possibilities of that statement, the good-looking guy shot Hank a glare before sharing another stunning revelation. "Sometimes my husband spends far too much time in his factory and with his sometimes-crusty father. I'm TJ. It stands for Timothy James. No one but my mother can get away with calling me that, though. And like any decent Texas child, I know if she spews out my full name, something bad is about to happen. Our daughter has already learned that. Our two-year-old son hasn't quite grasped the severity of that concept yet, however."

Before Seth could respond, Hank glared at his spouse. "And what TJ left off was that he is a partner at the leading civil rights law office in Texas. No one calls him anything but Mr. Hayes."

TJ shrugged but seemed unrepentant. "What can I say? I've always hated bullies, whether it was from the mouth of an eight-year-old whose father was KKK to…well, the parent of said child. They may not have a clue about the problem with white privilege, but I make sure there's a stiff cost."

TJ flushed an impressive shade of red and turned to Hank. "Sorry, hon. I promised to stay off my soapbox. I was too close to the pulpit just then."

Hank pulled TJ in and gave him a quick kiss. "Your passion is one of your best traits." Hank then took over the conversation. "So, before something else happens, I'd like to hire you as the advertising company for Hill Country Root Beer"—Hank lit up the room with a Cheshire cat grin—"and other assorted beverages from the glory days of soda fountains."

Seth shook his head. "You understand that there is no firm? It's just me and that oversized desk huddled in the corner of the living room."

The pair shared a conspiratorial glance then Hank said, "I'm sure you can find help. I understand a major firm in Fort Worth has recently folded. Besides, you're who we want to work with. And there will be lots of money for you thrown into this campaign once we're all comfortable with a dynamic new approach for all we want to do."

Seth tried to control his reaction to Hank's comments. He *was* searching for a new job. "Okay, you have a point. But there's no way I can have a serious business talk in a pair of gym shorts and the rattiest T-shirt I own."

"Hey, Hank! How's it been hanging?" Travis said, coming through the front door.

Seth didn't think he'd ever been so glad to see him. It gave Seth a chance to digest all the new facts and crazy possibilities that were springing from the recent revelations.

"Hey! How are you doing, Travis? Long time no see," Hank said.

"Kind of busy. A little theater here, a touch of drama there—enough to keep us out of trouble and the old ticker going." Then Travis paused, seeming to take note of the stranger in the room. "Who's the hot guy with you today? He's out of your league."

This time Seth wanted to slip underneath the couch and hide from the world. Travis didn't get the subtlety of navigating a million-dollar deal and he might have just offended his next meal-ticket.

"Travis, knock it off," Seth said. "This is Hank's husband, TJ. They are here to talk about me working with them on their account again."

Travis just grinned, now shaking hands with TJ. "Relax, Seth. Hank knew I was pulling his chain, and he *is* also smart enough to want you to create their new ad campaign. Who else could handle the Hill Country Root Beer vision for the century?" He cut Seth a glance, clearly just taking a good look at him. "For God's sake, Seth, did you just crawl out of bed? Why don't you get into some decent clothes? I'll keep the guys entertained with my great humor and wit."

Seth started to fume but realized Travis had given him the perfect out. *But what is he during home anyway?* Seth's curiosity got the better of him. "I thought you were gone for the day on a trip to East Texas?"

"They had a hell of a storm at the piney woods last night, so I had to cancel. Go, get dressed and show them how brilliant you are."

Seth darted for the bedroom while the three men moved to the shaded west porch. As he walked, he could catch bits of the ongoing chatter.

Travis isn't the backwoods fool he pretends he is. I'm sure he's schmoozing with the million-dollar client with no hesitation. I remember how much help he was to me when we toured their factory.

He ducked into their room, almost moving at a trot, stripping to nothing as he clicked the door shut. A few minutes later he had donned the uniform he'd worn for the past he-didn't-know-how-many years — khakis, a polo shirt and Skechers. He checked himself in the mirror, running his fingers through his hair.

Well, I let that get too long, but even Travis couldn't buy me the time to sneak into town for a haircut this morning.

He moved to the back door and the sounds of raucous laughter. Seth waited for several minutes, watching the three obviously enjoying each other's company. He realized, however, that it was his turn to perform at the 'Travis and Seth dog-and-pony show'.

He stepped onto the porch and smiled at everyone. "So, what were you thinking about us doing together? There were some ideas being floated around before the firm closing that we had planned to discuss that day we discovered the notices on the office door, so those might be a good place to start."

With Hank's agreement, Seth ducked back into his office area to grab some supplies and his notes from the account. Then he passed around pads of paper and handfuls of sharpened pencils. He patted himself on the back that he kept them on hand out of habit. He included Travis and TJ in the brainstorming session, as well. The two of them belonged at the table as much as Hank and he did.

The day passed from morning to dusk before they had finished working out the details of a first campaign. Travis had stayed through the whole event, as had TJ, although both of them had stepped out for phone calls a few times. But now they had reached the point where Hill Country Root Beer had a face. All Seth had to do was gather the people he needed to fill out the rest of the required talent. He needed a designer and a copywriter. He might hire someone he'd worked with before or get a graduating designer from one of the local colleges. He'd heard good things about North Texas. He realized that he was drifting in his own fog and should deal with all of that later, after his new client left.

"So, what are you doing these days, besides bailing out people that need a fresh eye on their products?" asked Hank.

Travis grinned then dropped into a presentation as impressive as anything Seth had seen in the last few years. The realization of what Travis had so effortlessly begun to do came to him as a bit of a shock. *He's pitching the rodeo school!*

Travis was on a roll. "So, I'll be working to diversify our brand. We're already including the obvious things — farm-to-table occasions, other seasonal events — and we've even discussed the whole dude-ranch thing. But we didn't think any of them were enough, either alone or in a combination. Then there is funding. They would require more starting monies than what we have available in ready cash."

Hank and TJ were leaning forward, clearly absorbing the ideas Travis shared. "So, what are you thinking? Forgery? Counterfeiting? Arranging for a monthly go-go show with performers brought from Dallas? Any other schemes you're hitting up?" TJ asked, clearly tongue-in-cheek.

This time Seth had the luxury of relaxing into his chair and seeing how Travis dealt with the barrage of questions, especially since TJ seemed to have the same smart-ass sense of humor as Travis did. But after a few seconds pause for the right words, Travis launched into a more complete overall plan.

"We were considering starting a rodeo school. We already have most of the facilities to teach bull riding, barrel racing and pole bending. But like we were saying, while we might have enough interest for the first session, it'll take more upfront money. The bank thinks we're a high-risk loan application too."

TJ snorted with amusement. "I can't imagine why. An unemployed advertising executive and a rancher starting a brand-new enterprise during one of the worst seasons of drought we've seen in, what, fifteen-years? I don't see that as risky at all," TJ said in his now-familiar satire-loaded voice.

"I don't know. It all seems pretty well planned out," Hank said. He caught TJ's gaze and the two of them locked in silent communication. When they turned to share their thoughts with Seth and Travis, their eyes twinkled like the proverbial kids in the candy store.

"So, have you thought about going for corporate sponsorships? If you're having a miniature rodeo at the end of each class session, that would put a sponsor in a great position to spread their brand on everything. It seems like an attractive proposition to me." He smiled at Travis.

Travis sat still for several seconds and even Seth found himself without a response. Travis started a number of times before making a helpless motion.

Seth said, "It's up to you, Travis. But it might be an angle to get some money in a way we hadn't thought about." *And I should have been the one to think of it first, since advertising is my field.*

Travis nodded, studying each of them. After a few seconds he seemed to have reached a consensus with himself. "We'll need to work out the details, but I would say Hill Country Root Beer is our premier corporate sponsor." Then he turned to Seth. "As owner of a new ad firm who represents them" — he winked at Seth — "I'd say your number one client needs to expand their brand to the rodeo game."

* * * *

Travis stood under the shower's hundred stinging sprays, letting it wash away some of the weariness of the day's activities. As he went through the motions, he smeared his body with a thick layer of bath soap, enjoying the sensations that washed over him. Travis teased his nipples then leaned back against the shower wall and explored his body, reaching down to stroke his lather-coated cock. He became harder with each pass and his desire grew until he heard the door open, then close. Someone was in the room with him, and he knew who he hoped it would be.

He also hoped that this wasn't another of those times when his desires and the possibilities of the moment would not align for the activities he had in mind.

Travis wiped the fog off the shower glass and smiled. His timing was better than usual. He peered out to see Seth bend over, his deep red briefs stretching over the muscular globes of his butt.

"You've got a sweet piece of ass there, my friend, but is this a good time to start something?" Travis asked.

Seth shoved his underwear down to his ankles, exposing the hair-lined crack that Travis had always found sexy. He liked his men on the natural side. Seth reached back and popped an ass cheek with each work-roughened palm. "The kids are with Dustin and Shane, planning for the weekend...something Dustin and Shane cooked up. They're hoping for Zane and Amy to teach at their school and they are somewhere working out the details—but that doesn't matter. What matters is we're here alone and I plan to screw you every way from Sunday."

"Oh? Is that how you see this going down?" Travis said.

"Yes, that is how I see this going down. And when they do go to teach, we'll have a week to do the wild thing. I have every intention of taking advantage of their trip to the other side of the state when it happens. But for now, we have a small window of opportunity."

Seth stalked to the shower, licking his lips with a clear indication that he was ready to put his plan into motion. He opened the door and steam billowed out into the room. Seth stepped in beside him and ran his hands over Travis. A few passes of his rough hands had Travis to a point of urgent and hungry desire. He groaned as Seth's teasing had his cock as hard as granite.

But Travis had no intention of standing passively while Seth drove him to a new level of delirium. He wrapped his arms around Seth, held him tight then ground their lips together and plunged his tongue into Seth's hot mouth. The steamy embrace allowed no doubt of his intentions.

Travis trapped his lover's face between his hands, devouring the man as if he were a hungry lion and Seth was his meal. The desire he had for Seth built with each touch.

Seth ran his palms down Travis' muscular back then cupped each butt cheek. He pulled them apart, clearly seeking a prize, then teased Travis' opening with slow deliberation. The soap and water combination running down Travis' back worked as a serviceable lube. Seth drew a finger over Travis' opening again then again, pressing a little harder each time.

Travis became obviously more desperate, moaning and pushing back against Seth's digit. Then suddenly Seth slipped his finger inside Travis to the first knuckle.

He paused, then worked it deeper with each rotation of his hand.

"Oh yeah, that's it. Finger-fuck me. Get me ready," Travis said as tremors of luxurious pleasure overtook him.

Seth laughed. "You're too eager. We need better lube than soap and water or else this will be the last fun we have for a while." He struggled to get himself to relax and enjoy Travis' idea of a reasonable pace.

Travis waited a few seconds before wrapping his hand tight around his cock and stroking himself. The ripple of sensations built inside him before he turned in the shower then ran his hands over Seth's chest, working on the hard nubs of flesh jutting out.

Travis drove his nails into Seth's nipples then twisted them, knowing how Seth enjoyed some things outside of vanilla. After he repeated the motion a few times, he had Seth moaning loud enough to almost vibrate the shower's tempered glass walls. Travis stepped forward, pinning Seth in the corner with water streaming over both of them.

He pressed against Seth, covering his lover like a quilt. As he nibbled down his neck, he whispered in Seth's ear. Before Seth could respond, Travis slid back Seth's foreskin and teased the underside of his cockhead. "Is that what you want? Is that how we'll make up for missed time?"

Seth snorted a few times before being able to reply. Travis wrapped his hand around their combined shafts and started stroking. The results were an explosive combination of electricity and fire. Seth began thrusting and their iron-hard dicks rubbing against each other sent Travis into the heights of pleasure.

He was racing toward climax when Seth pulled away, grabbed Travis and threw him over one shoulder. Travis squealed in response, but the next thing he knew his still-dripping body lay across their bed, coated with droplets of water.

"Hey, what are you doing? You're soaking the bed and everything on it."

"And you care?" Seth asked.

Travis considered for a second before laughing. "It'll be over a hundred today and so dry that we're under a burn ban. I guess I should keep in mind that everything's going to be dry almost instantly and just enjoy myself."

Seth lunged, grabbed Travis by the balls and pulled them tight. Travis' thought process shut down at that point. He wanted more of what Seth was dishing out.

"I thought you were talking too much, focusing on what you shouldn't be. Now, do you care that I left you dripping wet?"

Travis lay gasping for air and knew he couldn't care less. He just wanted Seth to keep doing what he'd been doing.

In response to Travis' silence, Seth spread the cowboy's knees apart. He was breathing in gasps when a stone-hard cock touched the underside of his butt. Travis felt as if he were plugged into enough power to light up a Christmas tree.

He started to chuckle just as Seth swallowed his dick up to his hairy crotch. Any coherent thought abandoned Travis at that point. For the next few minutes his world swirled with passion as Seth worked him over in ways he had not imagined possible a few months before. He was far past anything analytical about what Seth was doing to him because Travis was sending him soaring into the heights of pleasure.

The familiar sensation started building in Travis. Soon he couldn't hold back and he didn't care. He gasped when Seth pulled off his cock.

"Oh man, don't leave me like this. I'm so close. You've got me with a boner so hard that it makes my balls ache."

"You get to come when I say you can and not a moment before." Seth let out a deep growl. He grabbed Travis behind the knees and rolled him higher up onto his shoulders, exposing his tight hole. Seth darted in, flicking his tongue down the center of his ass and ran the tip of his tongue over Travis' opening.

"Oh fuck. Yes. *More.* Do more of *that.*" Travis was experiencing waves of euphoria that were overwhelming.

"You enjoying yourself?" Seth said between licks.

"Too much talking. Get busy. Need you in me."

Seth complied and began working his tongue into Travis' ass. Travis tensed, lost in the feelings zipping through his body. It didn't take long before he'd need more. As his muscles shivered with delight, Travis realized that Seth had retrieved the bottle of lube out of the nightstand.

Travis shivered when Seth coated his fingers and ran them along the crack of his ass. He sighed as Seth added even more of the slick before he pressed his thick digit inside. Travis fought to relax, but the finger being driven home made it almost impossible. A few seconds later, Seth hit his sweet spot, and the noise Travis made nearly shook the photographs on the wall.

Travis let out a breath and sighed. "Well yes…like that."

Seth said nothing but continued to work on Travis, thoroughly prepping him. Before long Seth had three fingers buried deep inside him. Travis was sprawled across the bed, his body twitching and nearly overwhelmed with waves of pleasure as Seth finger-fucked him, hitting his prostate on every thrust.

"Come on. Quit teasing me," Travis whined.

With the final push of his fingers, Seth pulled out then moved between Travis' spread legs. He ran his cockhead up and down Travis' ass, and Travis ground and twisted under Seth, groaning. Then Seth found his opening and pushed against Travis' hungry hole until his steel-hard cock slipped into Travis' grasping channel.

He wrapped his legs around Seth's torso, digging in his heels and acclimating to the delicious pleasure of being entered. Seth paused with attention that Travis appreciated. He was clearly waiting, giving him time to get past the wash of pain and pleasure engulfing him.

When Travis nodded his readiness for Seth to proceed, he grabbed Travis by his thighs and held on tight. He ground his crotch against Travis' ass. Then he readied Travis for a pounding he hoped he'd receive.

Travis could not do more than lose himself in the passion Seth created. He was lust-filled at a level Travis had experienced only on rare occasions.

Seth thrust inside him, leaving Travis lost in the wonderful sensations. He fought with the bedding surrounding him, unable to do more than groan in pleasure. Seth pulled almost all the way out before ramming back inside, giving Travis what he'd needed. Travis lost himself, thrashing under Seth as his pleasure grew.

"That's it. Keep it up. Are you gonna fuck the cum out of me?"

An uncharacteristic grin flashed across Seth's face. He reached up and put his hand over Travis' mouth. "No dirty talk. You aren't good at it. It kills the mood."

Before Travis could become offended, Seth drove his pounding thrusts to a higher level. Now Travis was reaching the point of no return. He dug his fingernails into Seth's back, writhing like a wild animal.

Suddenly Travis' body seized, his limbs locked around Seth. He felt Seth sink deeper until they both trembled, realized they had reached a mutual climax and relished the sensation. Travis' balls drew tight against him as the first of Seth's semen filled his ass, the white-hot cum signaling his climax. After what seemed like forever, Travis' muscles tensed with a final delicious wave, and an instant later, they collapsed together as the last spurt of Seth's cum flowed into him.

Seth crumpled on top of Travis and wrapped his arms tight.

"Don't we need a towel?" Travis asked.

"Not this time. I'll clean us up after our nap. I think it's kind of sexy."

Seth spooned with Travis. He drew a sheet over them and Travis let the gentle heat lull him into sleep.

* * * *

The next moment of awareness Travis experienced was the sound of Amy yelling through the house. "Dad. Hey, Dad. Shane and Dustin want to take us out to dinner."

Tangled in the sheet, Travis startled so badly that he fell out of bed as he struggled to recover. He realized that they'd left their bedroom door wide open.

Travis heard Zane call out, "Amy! I wouldn't go in there. Wait a minute."

The next thing Travis knew, she was standing in the doorway with Seth trying to cover himself in bed and Travis peering over the bed with a sense of horror.

Amy muttered, "Oh, shit…"

Zane appeared next, wearing a smirk. "What have you always told me about closing the door during private moments?" he asked.

Seth shot Zane a look that let Travis know they had already discussed sex and its many ramifications. It seemed he and Amy would be doing that now.

"Zane, please take Amy to the patio and get everyone something to drink." He waved his hand with some enthusiasm when he heard a hearty chuckle coming from the other room. *So now Shane and Dustin know what just happened. Great.* "Close the door, too. We'll be out in a minute."

Travis considered for a second and added, "Dinner is on us tonight."

Zane guided Amy away and closed the door behind them. As soon as the latch clicked shut, the men bounded to their feet. Travis started straightening the room and motioned to Seth.

"Get in the shower first. I'll change the sheets. It won't take long."

Seth stepped close and took Travis in his arms. "They know. I'd already talked to Zane about the fact that I'm bisexual. He's a bright kid. He'd already put together the pieces. You need to talk to Amy before we do anything else." He gave a knowing smile. "Also, we can shower together. It'll be faster."

Travis nodded in agreement and let Seth lead him into the shower where all this had started hours before. Soon they had slipped on clean clothes and polished boots. Travis ran his hands down his torso as he turned before the full-length mirror. He glanced at Seth.

"Do I look okay?"

Seth studied him for a minute before nodding. "You look great, but your expression looks like you've been eating sour pickles. Go. Talk to Amy." He closed his eyes for a moment then shook his head. "I'll keep my son and Dustin from firing off one-liners…if I can."

Travis led the way to the outdoor kitchen. Once they entered, Amy never gave him a chance to give his well-practiced speech.

"Come on, Dad. We need to talk." She turned and walked him back into the house, and this time he made sure the door closed behind them. He sat on the arm of one of the massive recliners and waited. Her barrage wasn't long in coming.

"Is this why Mom left? Because you decided you were *gay*?"

So that's her play. Travis was surprised and just a bit upset. "First, that isn't the reason your mother took off. I told her before we married that I was bi. She was okay with it. I thought you understood that too. That was a cheap shot. Now, the second thing… You know better. No one *decides* they will be gay. It doesn't work that way. I'm sorry it embarrassed you. I wasn't too happy about it either. It sure wasn't how I wanted to come out about our relationship to you. But it happened, and now Zane and Dustin will be teasing us for the rest of our lives."

"Shane, too."

"What?"

Amy's lips turned into a soft smile. "Shane was teasing Seth too."

"Great, and Seth will give me crap too."

"Knock it off," Amy said sternly.

Travis tensed. "Not off the hook yet, I take it."

"Not even close. You know I don't enjoy being left out of important conversations."

"Next time you'll be in the loop. I promise."

Amy slowed her pacing until she came to a stop in front of him, her arms crossed. She glared at him for a few seconds then eased them to her sides.

"Do you like Seth?"

"Honey, I think I may be in love."

Amy's expression soured, and he braced himself. "Would you do me a favor then?"

He nodded, his mouth going dry.

Her giggle was genuine. "Put a lock on your bedroom door — and use it."

Travis joined her in laughter. "Consider it done."

"Good. Now, did I remember something about the steaks being on you?"

Travis gave his daughter a hug and threaded his arm around her waist.

"Sounds delicious, but I may need to drive alone."

"Why's that?" said Amy.

"It may be the only way to survive the teasing."

"Yeah, what the heck were you thinking? I mean, that scene is forged into my brain forever." She vaulted out of range as he tried to swat her, then they raced toward the rest of the group.

Chapter Eight

Travis and Seth had been watching the weather for the past week. But what had started out as a glimmer of hope to break the drought was becoming fear of a major tropical storm as it churned through the Caribbean Islands and up the gulf, dumping floods of massive proportions.

Typically, a weather front of this sort didn't track as far north as they were, but nothing about the pending storm seemed normal. It was falling into the categories of 'epic' and 'disastrous', never terms Travis wanted to hear related to bad weather headed in their direction.

Travis understood that Seth would be there for moral support. Oh, he would help when the time came, but he hoped that moment might never happen. Right now, it was all guess and speculation, which wasn't Travis' strong point. "So, any suggestions on what we should do?" he asked.

Seth considered for a few moments. "Hard to tell. The storm's just sitting there at this stage, although the meteorologists have been talking about Galveston

Island being wiped out. We're far enough away, and the forecast is fluctuating. Who knows? We may not even get an inch of rain."

Travis cocked his eyebrow and studied Seth. "Whatever we need to do, it will be easier since there are four of us—plus James and Troy. If we have to do some sandbagging, I'm sure we can. I don't see where it's doing any good worrying about what might be. 'Might be' is a long way from it becoming a hurricane and hitting here. They haven't even started evacuating Houston."

"They have suggested it, though. I think the terminology the governor used was '*We* strongly *recommend you seek shelter to the north*,' or words to that effect," Seth said. "So what should we do? We need some kind of plan. At least it would make you feel better if we had one."

Travis' anger started to flare, but then he realized Seth was offering a valid suggestion. The more prepared he was, the less likely it was that the circumstances would catch him unawares. He considered for a few seconds more, but then was on his way in a fast walk to the dining room table. He dove into his stash of drafting supplies. It would be a great way to map out whatever they could do to prepare for this weather and where to put in the sandbags. He and Seth sat next to each other and dragged out the large map that covered the whole ranch. His spread included several miles of pastures with a large creek bisecting one third of it. There were bigger ranches, but not too many in the region this close to the metroplex. They worked on options, letting a good portion of the afternoon slip away without them noting its passage.

But as the hours passed, the forecast became more pointed. The storm was growing more ominous as it moved closer and its outer bands were beginning to arrive. The sky to the south of the ranch was the color of blacktop in July and it writhed and churned like the creek during a spring cloudburst. Travis began wondering if this would be more serious than even what the local forecasters were saying. Travis and Seth opened the radar screen on the computer. They stared at the spiral of reds and purple that seem to cover the gulf from off the coast of Padre Island to Houston.

"The forecast is for a bad hurricane. They're calling it 'the storm of the century' now. I guess that would be bad," Seth said.

He was studying the information when yells shattered the relative tranquility of the house. Zane and Amy were trying to find them, and they apparently wanted to find them *now*.

"Zane! Amy! We're in the dining room. Calm down. What are you so worked up about?"

Zane addressed the question as they bounded through the door. "Have you peeked outside? Do you know what's coming? They started a mandatory evacuation notice on all the towns from Corpus Christi up to Galveston. It's not gonna be good. They said we can get up to twenty inches of rain."

Travis was still, this time the portrait of calm. Seth's level of panic seemed to scale closer to that voiced by the kids. But as Travis rose, went to the entry hall and sat on the bench, slipping on his work-boots, a flash of lightning lit up the whole interior of the house.

"Holy shit!" he said.

In the instant before the glow disappeared, Travis started the internal countdown of the thunder that would follow. With each millisecond that he waited, he dreaded the response even more. Then came the boom of matching thunder. The lights in the house flickered, as an apocalyptic moment descended on them. Travis understood that the hurricane or whatever was definitely a major storm.

With the first explosion of thunder, it was clear that they all had to move into action. The wind shifted one-hundred-and-eighty degrees. The conditions around the ranch changed from gentle summer breezes to a torrent of gale-force winds burrowing into any opening. Travis turned to the other three. "Get the animals into the pens closer to the house where they have shelter, then tie, bolt and chain everything down. They're saying as much as hundred-mile-per-hour winds, and they could be higher. At that speed, everything becomes a dangerous projectile."

Travis jumped when the back door opened with a violent crash against the doorframe. Silhouettes filled the space as lightning struck once more, backlighting the two people standing in the opening. This time the thunder was not as loud, Travis didn't feel it as deep in his bones as he had the clap before. After it passed, he saw that James and Troy were the ones who had joined them. With no prelude, James fell into a rapid narrative.

"First, the leading edge of some of the strongest storm bands is not very far away from us. Troy and I moved some breeding stock closer so they can get into the barn. The other herds I drove across the creek in case we flood. I was thinking we need to have everything tied down and as close to the house as we can get it."

The two stood for a moment as if waiting to see if they had done what Travis would have wanted. To their credit, they had. It was more or less a battening down of the hatches and preparation for the storm on the high seas, only this time the tremendous seas were the prairies of Central Texas.

"Great work, James. Take the ATV to do what else you need to do. I don't think the horses should stay out in the pouring rain. We don't want to have to worry about lightning striking too close to a horse, have him spooked and buck one of you off. All we need is an injury amid all this chaos."

James picked up the narrative from Travis' start. "I'll take Troy with me. We can work the rest of the cattle without horses. They'll want to move into some place more sheltered than the creek bottom, so it won't be too hard."

Without further discussion, Travis turned to the other three. "Start putting everything away, chain down the equipment..." Travis took a deep breath, realizing he was repeating himself to people who didn't need any instruction.

"Everyone make sure you have your mobiles. If the storm hits the tower, we may not have Internet or phone. But from the maps I studied, we only have about a thirty-minute head start before the first wave slams into us."

Zane studied the computer screen and saw the pinwheel moving toward their part of the country. He let out a low whistle. "This is bad. Really bad."

"Agreed. Now we need to get moving." With that directive, they started spilling out of the house toward their appointed tasks.

* * * *

The time had slipped away until the overall question changed to one of saving the buildings. Then everything became more pessimistic and flipped to wondering how bad it would get. The environment that had kept them safe for the past hundred years was now suspect. Travis began to wonder where the ground was high enough to be safe. But before they'd even finished the last of their tasks, the first tendril of the hurricane unleashed itself.

The trees whipped back and forth. Travis didn't know if the century-old elms that surrounded the house could survive undamaged. Big branches swayed with a violence he'd never seen. They had secured the last of the outdoor kitchen when he saw Zane and Amy charging through the drenching rain. Amy caught a violent gust and staggered.

Travis started to run out into the storm to rescue his daughter, but Zane reached her first and held tight. The scene recalled memories of dustbowl farmers huddled against the storms. Zane helped her until they were on the patio, which lessened the ferocity of the winds swirling around them.

Seth was the first one to bring up the question that was troubling Travis. "Where are James and Troy? If they don't make it back across the creek soon, the water may be too high."

"There's no telling where they are. They were covering a lot of area. It's pouring now too. I doubt we could find them. Once this line of storm passes, we'll be able to locate them."

It became obvious Travis had made a good call when about thirty minutes into the current torrent of rain there was a break that allowed them to assess the situation. They were fortunate enough to still have Internet.

He and Seth jumped into the closest four-wheel-drive pickup and cut across flooding pastures until he came to the final ridge before reaching the creek. When he topped the rim, he slammed on his brakes. Water filled the horizon and was within a few inches of lapping at his front tires. Travis' gut twisted, and he found it difficult to swallow.

Where their typical peaceful stream had flowed, providing relief for cattle on the ranch for the last hundred years, a violent torrent of unprecedented floodwater overwhelmed the landscape. It was no longer a passive feature that made Travis feel like he was home. It had morphed into a roaring deluge that filled far beyond its banks. The flooding was epic, due to the drought causing the ground to be packed too hard for the rain to absorb. That, along with the rain pouring, didn't give the water a chance to seep into the parched ground, so it was running wild.

But that wasn't the worst of the situation, because when he scanned the far side of the expanse, he saw a three-sided shed they had put in the pasture to protect a salt lick.

That shed was now an island and he could see no way for him to rescue the pair of men who were at least a quarter of a mile away and struggling to climb onto its roof. They didn't have much time. Travis knew from the weather maps they'd been studying that this had only been the first band of the storm, and there would be many more to follow. Each of them seemed to have the same devastating potential or more. Time was short and Travis was at a loss. He was struggling to think of a way to recover James and Troy when a black pickup skidded to a stop beside them. Amy and Zane bailed out of the truck and ran to Travis, quickly taking in the dire situation.

"We have to get them out. The water's rising even faster down here." She turned to her father with pleading eyes. "What are you going to do?"

Travis waited for a few seconds, trying to make his kaleidoscope of thoughts congeal in a way that something useful might come from them. Then he remembered a conversation he'd had recently with TJ about an odd hobby the lawyer had. At least at the time it had seemed odd, but right now it looked like the path to salvation.

With any luck, he will be the hero of the day.

Travis tapped on TJ's phone number from his list of contacts, keeping a positive outlook despite the persistent crackling noises coming through his cell. Then the signal strength grew and gave Travis hope.

"Travis?" TJ answered.

With no hesitation, Travis launched into an explanation of his needs. "TJ, didn't you tell me you had an airboat you play with on the weekends?"

Travis set the speaker option on his phone and everyone held their breath while they waited for TJ to reply.

"Hell yes, I still have the airboat. It's in good shape, too. I just had it serviced because sometimes I get called in for water rescues. What's wrong?"

Travis was almost in tears. "We have two people stranded on the roof of an outbuilding, and there's a lake between us and them."

"Have someone waiting at the gate. We'll need a guide. I don't want to lose a second of time getting to them. The next band of the storm is only a few hours away."

In what seemed like days but was no doubt less than an hour, Travis spotted TJ coming over the hill with an airboat bouncing along on a trailer behind him. Hank was standing in the pickup's bed, swinging his arms, yelling something ridiculous.

'Root beer! Root beer! We got root beer. Now we're gonna save your ass with good old-fashioned root beer. Root beer! Root beer!'

Zane was in the passenger seat with a big grin on his face. That made Travis happier than he'd been since this disaster had begun.

TJ orchestrated the unloading of the boat and soon it was floating in only a few inches of water while TJ secured his life vest. He snapped the buckle and motioned the group closer.

"I only have room for one more person. Who is it going to be?"

Travis stepped forward, answering the question by beginning to put on the life vest. Seth took him by the arm and pulled him around so their eyes met. "You sure that's a good idea? I swim better than you."

"It's my fault they're there. I sent them to work the cattle in that part of the ranch. Now I have to get them out." Travis moved to the seat beside TJ, took the headphones and put them in place.

"Ready?" TJ asked.

Travis barely got out a response before TJ accelerated the boat and it skimmed across the water like a flat stone over the pond on a calm summer day.

Then a second later he demonstrated his piloting skills. Mostly it had been him trying to keep from hitting brush or trees that were visible. But after a few minutes, Travis was questioning his sanity as he wondered about TJ's seemingly manic energy. *This is what he does for fun?* But it became obvious soon enough that TJ was a skilled operator. He covered the distance without issue.

Once they were close enough, he motioned to Travis and yelled over the whine of the giant fan.

"I can slide onto the roof of the shed. It's almost even with the bottom of the boat. We need to get both of them in life vests before we chance the rescue. I don't like the odds, and I want the highest possibility of success.

TJ maneuvered the boat a few times, making it close enough for Travis to toss James and Troy safety vests that he hoped they didn't need. Then he finessed the boat until a skilled acceleration pushed them to the unoccupied part of the shed's roof. It rocked for a moment then settled into place.

Travis motioned them toward the boat. "This may be our best chance to get you. Hurry, but don't fall. Whatever you do, don't fall."

He felt TJ pop him on the shoulder a few times. When he glanced over, TJ gave him the sign to zip his lip. He realized he was saying too much, which might make them more prone to panic. TJ motioned again to Travis. "Use the ropes. Throw one end to them if you have to."

Travis nodded his understanding and found the coiled rope under his feet. He moved around until he caught Troy's attention. Once he knew they could hear, he yelled out instructions to the pair.

"Troy, you go first. Once we have you in the boat, we'll get your dad. Got it?"

There was a brief hesitation and the pair argued. But James made a motion any father would recognize, followed with a bellowed order.

"Go!"

Once Troy positioned himself as close as he could, Travis threw him the rescue line. A gust of wind caught it and it fell a few feet short. Questioning his ability to accomplish the rescue, he turned to TJ. This time he got more guidance.

"Aim upstream. The rope will float. You can do this," TJ said.

Travis cast the line again, and this time Troy grabbed it. After securing the rope to his life vest, the boy began to edge across the galvanized metal roof. They were within inches of each other when his boot slipped and a split-second later Troy was on his hands and knees, his expression the definition of abject terror.

"It's all good. Only a little farther. Just grab my hand," said Travis.

Troy nodded, locked his gaze on Travis and crawled. Those inches were some of the longest Travis had ever suffered through. Once he knew their hands were close, he lunged. It was one of the best sensations he had experienced in recent memory when Troy grabbed tight, braced against the boats side and heaved. Nothing moved for several seconds, then Troy's weight shifted and he lay in the boat's bottom like a prized marlin.

Travis started to celebrate but heard TJ.

"Travis."

He followed TJ's gaze and his blood ran cold. The water had risen while he'd been busy getting Troy. Now the creek was a few inches over the shed roof, and James' face said it all.

"Dad!"

He spun to Troy. "Untie yourself. We'll have him in the boat in a second."

He twirled the rope over his head like it was among the finest in rawhide lariats. It found its way across the space, and at the last second, James jumped for it. Time froze for Travis as he watched. He wasn't sure who had won when James landed in the water that was now covering the entire metal roof but was relieved when James rose, tying the rope to his vest. He tossed Troy the rest of the rope as he tightened his own grip.

"Pull!"

This time fear and adrenaline gave new power to the effort and near disaster was averted. They reached into the murky water, Travis and Troy grabbing James under an arm. Once he was in the boat, Travis yelled.

"Got him! Gun it."

The airboat hesitated for a second and a cold chill ran through Travis. Then the craft rocked, TJ gunned the motor and the boat broke free. Travis' nerves battled through the return trip. He could see the tension in the small party's faces as the boat escaped the heavy current.

The cheer of the crowd masked the roar of the boat's fan as TJ landed it. Zane and Seth helped Troy and James exit. Through all the hoopla, Travis stayed in his seat. He saw TJ and Seth coming toward him but couldn't bring himself to stand. It was as if his legs had turned to Jell-O. They both knelt beside him, giving him time to recover.

TJ spoke first. "It's overwhelming, isn't it? The whole 'saving people' thing."

This time Travis responded. "It is, and it could have all gone bad too."

TJ nodded "Could've...but didn't. Always remember that."

Travis shuddered and realized Seth was beside him. He grinned and wrapped his hands around Travis' arm. "Let's go to the house and I'll draw you a hot bath."

With a glint in his eye, TJ smirked at the rancher. "Being a hero makes me horny."

Hank covered his face with his hands. After a few seconds, Hank peered between his fingers. "And he's not kidding."

* * * *

Travis stood staring out of the window to the lake that his ranch had become in the last ten days of nonstop rain. The hurricane had found itself a nice comfortable spot and did what storms in history rarely had done. It stopped moving.

The initial shock left them battling against the weather. Families who had never had issues with the rainfall before were being rescued in boats similar to TJ's. The photographs and videos on television showed people stranded on their own roofs. They cut their way out through their attic then were lifted off by rescue helicopters before the houses could collapse and wash downriver. Even as the flood grew, the storm continued to make the situation worse.

So far, they'd driven in and out of the ranch on roads that already existed, but he wasn't sure how long that would last. As he watched, the rain started to increase in volume again. Travis became concerned that they had reached the end of possibilities for keeping the house from taking on water.

"Damn. It's raining harder?" James said from behind him.

Travis replied, "Feels like it. I was hoping to catch a break today. The runoff doesn't seem to be finding drainage, but it would be nice if I were wrong."

"Yeah, that would be fantastic. If nothing else, I wanted to see how much storm damage we sustained at our house."

Travis worried about losses at James' house too. They'd built it for Travis' family in the earlier years of the homestead. But the family's needs had grown, and it had become the ranch manager's place. The one good thing about the house James and Troy lived in was that it had flood insurance, and they'd already stored most of their belongings in the barn's loft. Travis' father had made that decision and Travis had maintained the coverage. His dad had thought the house was too close to one of the smaller branches of the creek that ran through the entire ranch. Travis remembered his dad telling him, '*The rest of this ranch is too high to flood, but we managed to plant that house in the one spot where a few extra drops of water might cause trouble. I don't want to fight with Mother Nature. You always lose when you piss off that uppity bitch.*'

Travis saddened as he thought of his parents. His father had suffered a stroke when he'd been sixty while he'd been walking between the house and the barn. Travis had heard an odd sound, and his dad had collapsed like someone had cut the strings on a marionette. The doctor had told him it was a massive stroke and that he'd likely never known what happened.

His mother had never recovered from losing the love of her life. Six months later he'd lost her too. She'd never woken up one morning. The doctor had said it was a heart attack, but Travis had always known what it had been—heartbreak. She couldn't stand to not be with his dad.

Travis had been adrift for quite some time after losing his parents. Even Amy could not console him. But like in all things, he'd had to choose his own path, knowing it would devastate his dad if they lost the ranch.

It drew Travis from his melancholy when Seth walked up beside him and handed him a cup of coffee. The two of them watched the now-steady rain.

"The cattle are okay, same for the horses. We let them into the pastures in the hills. If they flood, most of North Texas will be underwater," Seth said.

Travis nodded in agreement, doing the mental inventory of where everything was. Seth was right. Those pastures should have no problem staying below the flood waters. "I'm still worried about the house. I don't think any of us realized it was so vulnerable."

Seth motioned toward the wall of sandbags. They surrounded the house, protecting it, along with the pump that was spewing a three-inch-diameter stream of water out of what was becoming a moat surrounding the house.

"How much longer do we have? Over the last couple of days, we've bagged up most of the sand that we have. If the water goes over the top..." There was a significant expression on Travis' face. He knew that would be the final death knell for the ranch. The family had nowhere to go if the house was gone.

"It'll be enough. The creek drains into the Brazos. We will be fine." Seth took Travis by the arm, leading him into the kitchen where Amy and Zane were making breakfast. So far, they were in good shape for provisions. TJ had made that possible by more or less leaving his airboat at Travis and Seth's disposal for a couple of days, though he'd picked it up to help with the rescue effort right after. Although neither of them had any intention of trying to perform a rescue, it had given them a way to bring food over the flooded county roads to lay in supplies, and it had thrilled Zane to make runs to the highways in it.

Seth set a plate of eggs, bacon and biscuits in front of Travis with a smile.

"We'll go out in the rain and make damn sure we lose nothing, but first we have to eat. There aren't that many of us." There were nods of agreement from everyone, and Travis did not miss the determination. If they went under, it would be with a fight. He knew his dad was right, though. He wasn't gonna win a battle with Mother Nature. *All I can hope for is that she spares me.*

Travis jerked from his melancholy a short time later when he heard the growl of the diesel engine starting and the sound of the front-end loader's bucket hitting the water as James began moving the ranch's equipment, marking the beginning of the workday.

James drove the front-end loader to what was left of the pile of sand they'd received a few days before. He dropped the bucket, shoved forward a few feet to fill it then positioned the it as close as possible to the knee-wall that was keeping the rising water from invading the house. With grim determination, they begin to fill new ones. By splitting the work between the small group rotating in and out, they kept ahead of the still-rising water.

But filling fifty-pound bags and stacking them side-by-side was becoming exhausting to deal with. As they approached the time when they would need to rest and recover again, Travis realized he didn't have many choices left. It seemed like he would lose, and everyone who told him he was crazy for trying to save the house will have been right.

The lightning crackled again, sent in such a frequent display that it almost didn't register with Travis anymore. But it warned the beginning of another day of rising water and exhausting more supplies needed by the ranch. Even worse, they didn't have sand to last through the entire day. Seth walked up with more bags, his determination as strong as ever. Travis shook his head and motioned for him to stop.

"We have nothing much left to put in them, even if we weren't all exhausted and had more pumps. The flood got ahead of us."

Seth started to argue but must have realized it was futile. They'd run out of resources and there just weren't enough people to work non-stop hours to try to save the house. He sank his shovel into the ankle-deep water enclosure created with sandbags and leaned against Travis. Both of them stood staring at the lake surrounding the house.

Seth and Travis stopped with a sigh of resignation and braced themselves against whatever tool they had in their hand at the moment. The rumble of distant thunder became the cackle of Mother Nature when she knew she'd won the battle.

Seth leaned forward, turning his head to catch a sound. "What was that? Do you hear that?" He turned to Travis. "I hear an engine. It's not my imagination either. Listen…"

TJ came sliding to a stop in front of them, his boat packed with supplies and people. Travis glanced around and realized that he was being surrounded by boatloads of friends and acquaintances. Not only that, but someone had figured out how to get through the country roads with heavy equipment.

The convoy of dump trucks and loaders brought tears to Travis' eyes. The people jumped out of the boats and began forming a berm around the house as they filled sandbags.

To give them an even better chance of success, Travis thought the rain had slowed. Seth walked up beside him, smiling from cheek to cheek. He held up his smartphone to show Travis the radar.

"Look. I think this might save us. The National Weather Service is saying the last of the storm is breaking up. No more rain. It will take a few days to drain, but we're upstream so far that we should see the benefits of the end before anyone else." He studied Seth for a moment, then grabbed him and started pounding his back in celebration.

Travis couldn't believe how lucky he was to have the support of so many of the area folks who'd come to help him. And if the weather radar was right—and it should be—the nightmare should be over.

He walked through the crowd, shaking hands and hugging his saviors, but no one stopped working for long. And much to his surprise, several came back over the next few days just to make sure the sandbags were holding and the water was draining away properly.

A few days later found Travis surveying the results of the flood. It had taken more than a few days for the water to drain away completely and repairs to begin. The most severe destruction was on James' house. The horses and cattle had survived. The water hadn't damaged the rodeo arenas that had been under construction.

He sensed Seth walking up behind him and relished the hand that came to rest on his shoulder. "What do you think?"

"What do I think? I think I've witnessed a freaking miracle," Travis said with an enormous grin.

"Me too... Me too," Seth replied.

Chapter Nine

Seth sat in the bleachers, knowing that the work he and Zane had done on his riding skills for the last eight months would come to its conclusion over the next three days. His nerves were stretched to the point of breaking. His left leg jerked up and down like a box of nervous jackrabbits.

He watched his son, who was relaxed as he joked with the other bull riders. He would end up as the CEO of some major corporation. That was the goal they both were working toward — or at least the one Zane had voiced the most often. But the one thing that had to happen before any of those things could come to fruition was he had to win the state finals in bull riding and get that coveted scholarship from State.

"Hey, would you mind some company?"

Seth saw Travis trailing behind him and only a step or two farther back were Hank and TJ. It seemed the families had become more intertwined with each passing day. "Sure! Anytime... And I would love to have someone else take over some of my jittery nerves.

I don't care at this point who, as long as I can share some butterflies in my stomach."

The group chuckled and settled into the bleachers beside him. Travis wrapped his arm around Seth's shoulders and gave him a quick hug. As he released Seth, they shifted their attention to the competition.

Seth waved at the cluster of cowboys around the arena. This was different from the typical county fair. They were inside the dome and somehow that seem to change everything. The bulls worked their way into their chutes as the young men studied their draws. Once the bulls were in place, the cowboys started a familiar dance of securing ropes and fastening the bucking straps on each bull. Some of the animals were intense enough that they were trying to climb over the fences to get to somebody. Seth hoped Zane had not drawn any of those particular beasts.

"We're about halfway through today's rounds. There's been a few good runs. Some of the cowboys don't have the same experience of others."

"Yeah, but Zane's been doing this for years. I'm sure he'll do fine," said Travis.

Seth kept silent, but deep down that was his hope too. Regardless, they were ready for the next few days. He almost wished it were more like a regular sport where he could see the recruiters from various teams. There were thousands of people there, but Seth did not understand who the major players were from the colleges in the region.

TJ appeared in front of him and nodded. "I'm getting some drinks. What would you like?"

Confusion filled Seth. "They don't serve beer. It's a dry event. The Junior Rodeo Association decided that several years ago."

TJ patted Seth on the shoulder and chuckled. "That's fine. I wasn't going to get us hammered, anyway. But I thought I might check out the competition in the root beer category, if anybody was willing."

Seth tried to bring his thoughts together and waited for his embarrassment to retreat. "Okay, yeah… because my brain just assumed everyone needed the beer too. I'll take whatever you come back with. I'm not real picky."

Seth thought for a few seconds while TJ repeated his question and motioned to Seth again, this time with a smirk across his face. "Let me make myself clear. I'm good with anything except a bottle of Coke that is half-filled with redskin peanuts." He winked at Travis.

The laughter came naturally this time as Seth settled in to wait for Zane's round, and it wasn't much longer before they reached that point in the evening. Zane climbed onto his bull and settled in for his eight-second ride. The bull didn't seem too aggressive, but that wasn't as good a news as someone might think because half the score Zane would get was how impressive the bull was at trying to buck Zane off.

He could see the tension wash through his son as he finished his last-minute adjustments and double-checked his equipment. The time came that Seth had been waiting for. He reached over and grabbed Travis' thigh as a case of jitters overcame him.

The bull broke out of the chute with two hops that would score high. Then the brindle bull made a spin that was more reminiscent of a bull much older and more skilled than what Seth thought this one was, but Zane held on at every point of contact. His free hand was straight up, and his whole posture showed control over his ride. Then, unexpectedly, the animal sunfished, all four feet going into the air, and Zane tried to compensate for the maneuver.

Zane displayed skill that were beyond his typical ability, synchronous with the bull's impressive bucking. And as the seconds dribbled past, Zane met every challenge forced upon him by the bull. Seth thought Zane should score high.

An interminable amount of time passed before the buzzer sounded the end of Zane's ride. This time he didn't screw around with showboating his dismount, either. Zane used the next arching jump from the bull, propelled himself into midair, then hit the arena floor at a sprint.

He was running for the fence when the bull realized the person who had irritated him was free game. Seth gripped the edge of his seat, praying the animal would lose this race.

But he forgot to give the bullfighter his due, because from one side a bullfighter ran between Zane and the bull that had decided his job today was to fuck up Zane.

When the bullfighter sprinted between the two of them, the dangling strips of bright-colored cloth seemed to do their job. The bull snorted and came to a sliding stop as he tried to decide which was his true target. That second was all Zane needed to scramble over the fence. The bullfighter was playing for the crowd but monitored the young cowboy and knew when he was over the fence and safe.

Seth's friends descended on him, thumping his back and yelling at the top of their voices. He couldn't last long before a smile leaked its way across his face a few seconds later. And they were still in fine fettle when Shane called to them. "Calm down, guys. They're gonna throw us out of here." He winked at TJ and

Hank. "They'll never believe that all we had is a few bottles of root beer."

"Yeah, and it wasn't even good root beer — sure not Hill Country," Travis said, making Hank smile.

He draped his arms around the other two and squeeze them into a hug. "This is the point where Seth will make sure his baby boy didn't get injured, then we'll be waiting for the results of this ride and wait for the next one. It's classic nail-biting time. He'll be watching the other scores and seeing how Zane does compared to them."

Hank shifted between them and raised an eyebrow. "Everything seems fantastic to me. I used to do a little rodeoing, but I was in junior high when I stopped. I guess I'm just not enough of a daredevil to risk my skull against a two-thousand-pound bull every weekend."

They all laughed at Hank, knowing if there were ever any interaction between him and a large animal, there would be multiple strong fences between them.

If Hank wanted to avoid a bull, that was fine with Seth. He motioned to their clients and issued an invitation. "We're having steaks tonight. It's on us if you're interested. We thought we'd go to that new steakhouse. Zane and Amy made the choice. Her competition was in the afternoon."

"How did she do? She sounds so confident in her events."

"She did just fine. Didn't knock over any of the poles or the barrels. She just seems to have lost some of her fire. It's like she'd rather talk to Zane about bull riding. But she still has two years, and she's not a short-timer."

The pair nodded and Hank said, "Sounds great. We'll meet you at the steakhouse later, but we'll leave now" — he turned to address TJ — "otherwise you'll just sit here and watch the hot guys in tight Wranglers trail by." TJ gave Hank an unrepentant grin when he popped him on the back of the head for his comment. That ended the amount of small talk Seth could take before checking on his son.

Seth studied Zane as he reoriented himself for his next round. Everything here was different from what his son had competed in many times before. This wasn't some small-town county fair facility that needed paint and patching. This was an accommodation that could become whatever was called for, from Ice Capades to a rock concert to the State Junior Rodeo Championship, which was the role it was currently serving. Zane found a quiet spot, heaved his gear onto the fence and started re-dressing in the last of his safety equipment.

He had slipped on the Kevlar vest, then worked on the face guard and helmet that he wore for each match. Some people opted out of a lot of the extra gear Zane used, but Seth wouldn't ever give Zane the choice to do that. He couldn't see where his son risking being a mental vegetable for the rest of his life was worth not having any more protection on his head than a thin layer of felt shaped into a cowboy hat. Zane waved his helmet at his dad before he began to carefully snap the face guard in place and tighten down the buckles. He was ready for his last round.

The workers were putting bucking straps on the final group of bulls when a massive red bull with horns as long as Seth's forearms raced forward, slamming into the gate ahead of him like a runaway city bus. From the expression that developed on Zane's face, he was getting a warning.

Seth scrambled along the walkway, recognizing that bull was a nasty competitor and it was his son's ride

Seth's anxiety skyrocketed and he began the same routine of deep breathing and prayers that he put himself through the other thousand times Zane rode a bull. He had worked with others just as rank. Zane would do the ride to the best of his ability. It would go fine. There was no reason for Seth to let a bull with an attitude freak him out.

The cowboys surrounding Zane's chute started helping him. The first three times he tried to ease himself onto the bull's back, the bull tried to climb out of the chute and Zane had to bail off. Then, on his third attempt, the bull seemed to have decided to cooperate. In a few minutes, Zane was tightening his rope around the bull, the platter of bells still marking its movements. He coated the rope with enough resin to glue his hand in place. Zane hunkered down, waved his free hand well over his head and gave the gate man a quick nod.

Everything seemed to freeze in place for a few heartbeats. The bull exploded from the chute with a snorted war-cry. With the first jump, the animal landed on his front feet, almost twisting himself into a U-shape and flinging Zane in a way that challenged his grip. A few more of those bone-shaking maneuvers, and Seth was worried his son wouldn't make the eight seconds on this monster.

It froze, swinging its head as it sought a new target before launching into a whole series of attacks. By the third iteration, the bull had almost unseated Zane.

Then Zane made the move Seth dreaded seeing the most. His boy shifted to the inside of one of the torturous spinning moves that the bull had loosed on him. The bull somehow reversed his spin a few times until Zane seemed disoriented beyond recovery. It became a matter of his son living through the ride. The bull's last two kicks were high enough that Zane could have touched his tailhead. Zane shifted again, and again… At least he'd scored for part of the ride. Zane grabbed the rope with both hands, and his focus visibly became how to survive his time on a bull that was now trying to destroy him. He held on tight and Seth realized the resin had Zane's grip glued to the rope like a cheap Christmas toy. Seth's alarm grew until he spotted the bullfighters coming to help.

One of them launched himself at the bull and Zane tried to get his hand peeled off the rope. The bullfighter tugged a few more times, aiming to avoid the tangle of equipment. As Zane began to visibly panic, the bull-fighter slammed against the bull and there was a blessed moment when Zane's hand slipped free.

The bullfighter popped loose, his and Zane's boots hitting the ground simultaneously and him shoving Zane ahead of him. As Seth held his breath, the two of them focused on reaching the fence and escaping the terrifying animal hunting them down.

I have to do something.

Seth leaped up on a run, hit the wall of steel pipe and vaulted over the first fence. Zane was on the opposite side.

Seth grabbed Zane as he hit the top of the second fence and he yanked his boy over the rail. The two of them toppled to the ground together with their arms wrapped around each other. They separated enough for Seth to check on Zane.

"You okay? Is everything okay?" Seth said.

Zane started laughing hysterically, the tension ebbing as he slumped back into his father's arms.

"I'm okay. The bull tried to fuck me up, but he didn't get to." Zane waved his hand toward the arena where they were setting up for the cowboy after him. "But whoever that bullfighter is, I owe him a steak dinner, because he pulled my giblets out of the fire on that round."

"It was Shane. He was your guardian angel through this mess."

Seth realized that he and his son were the focus of the people in the arena. Zane bounced to his feet, turned to the concerned crowd and waved. Then he turned back to his dad and extended a hand to him.

But the announcer hadn't finished. When Seth could follow the words, he thought he would be sick. The announcement coming from the speakers shocked him.

"Hold on, folks. We have a flag on Zane Davis' ride. We are reviewing the video and will have the final results by the last run."

By the time the static of the speaker faded, Zane had collapsed against the railing. The friends who'd crowded around him were nothing more than a loud hum added to the overwhelming noise. The weight on Zane must be almost unbearable.

The last few contestants ran their rounds and a silence of dread settled over the small group. The results of the inquiry were announced.

"The video for Zane Davis was reviewed, and it was a unanimous decision by the judges that there was contact between the cowboy's free hand and the bull before the timer ended. The ride is a fault...zero points."

"Time for Plan B. Whatever the heck that is..." Zane said.

Seth wanted to hold his son and take away all the disappointment and pain.

Chapter Ten

Zane had been working all morning, going through the motions of getting stuff done. He was trying to pull himself together but didn't understand how to patch up the shards of his life's goal and move forward.

It didn't help that Zane had thought he was a sure thing for winning the scholarship. Now, their plans had been shot to hell in eight seconds. After spending the year chasing down winning rounds like notches on a dueling pistol—a solid year of sweeping round after round—it had all hinged on a final go on one vicious bull. Because of the fault round, Zane had come in second. But when they gave out the awards, it had crushed him to know they'd presented his biggest rival the title of state junior bull riding champion.

"Sorry, Zane. It was a hard loss. You were so close."

Zane glanced to his side, catching sight of his dad beside him. "Yeah, it sucks," Zane said. "All those years came down to one GD ride. It just shows that somebody up there has a wicked sense of humor about this whole thing." Zane cast a harsh glare skyward.

Seth shook his head. "It's nothing horrible. You can try for next year's scholarship. At least you didn't get hurt. That son-of-a-bitch bull you drew was out to tear you up."

Zane started to move away, giving his father a look that said it all. It was written across his face. Yes, he still had his health, and yes, he could maybe still go to school. The State scholarship hadn't been the only thing he had going for him. His dad had made certain to remind him of that regularly over the past week. He had been awarded a few small scholarships from local groups, but Zane was still so angry that it oozed from his pores, and he just didn't see how they could make school happen. He was upset at the unfairness of it all.

Everyone kept telling him that he would be okay, but Zane didn't just want to be all right. He wanted to relive that fateful ride and win the competition on the last go. He thought he should have won everything. That was how he'd felt since the final buzzer over a week before. Since then, the week had been a collection of little disasters that had only added to the overall sense of gloom. His dad had tried to bolster his ego. *'We'll still get you to college somehow. Everything will be fine.'* It sounded like a hollow promise.

Zane was about to lose control when, out of the corner of his eye, he saw a truck pulling to a stop in front of the house. He recognized the two occupants as the root beer guys. He studied the group for a second, then his dad turned to him with a puzzled, 'what are they doing here' expression. "Hang on. I'll be back."

As Seth walked over to the new arrivals, Travis followed them and they huddled around the pickup. If Zane's mood hadn't been so dark, he might have paid more attention. The conversation seemed to be changing to something much more dynamic when a few minutes later, his dad called over for him to join them.

Yeah, like I feel like making small-talk.

When Travis pointed him out, he knew something was going on beyond the typical client stuff. He made an internal shrug and headed toward where his dad and Travis stood with the two men from the beverage company.

"Morning. How are you doing?" Zane said. He cast a glance at his dad but all he got in reply was a shrug and a small smile.

One of the men began to explain. "First, I'm Hank and this is my husband, TJ. We've been working with your dad for the past several months." He paused and glanced at TJ, who gave him a quick nod.

"Zane, we have been talking about your scholarship and how that didn't work out the way you and your dad had hoped. But we're also the sponsors for the rodeo school your dad and Travis are creating. It needed some seed money, awarding a few scholarships for students who had been through the program and to support people who were teaching. It seemed like a good way to promote our product and the school."

Zane studied the crowd surrounding him. Everyone seemed to have a grin covering their faces. *So what does all of this have to do with me?*

Then TJ and Hank both focused on Zane.

"All right, all right. Enough tension. We want to give you a scholarship to cover part of your college expenses. Any school you want to attend. We'll match half for the entire time…all four years. That should give people a taste for the level of winners the school produces."

Seth waited to see Zane's reaction. When he did reply, it wasn't quite the excited way he'd hoped Zane would respond. "But I didn't go to the rodeo school. It isn't even open yet. So I don't see how it would help to give me a scholarship."

Seth did a face plant into his hand and groaned, while Zane's expression made it obvious that he realized this wasn't the best way to accept money. Hank's next words made Seth feel more relaxed, since it was obvious his son needed some refinement on business dealings.

"No," said Hank. "That's a valid question. And the answer is that Zane will be the spokesperson for the school. Also, he'll be one of the trainers in the bull riding events. Even coming in second in the state finals will impress a lot of people."

As they contemplated Hank's offer, a truck none of them had seen before drove up and parked. They all looked at each other, but Travis commented first. "I had nothing to do with this. Anyone else want to confess?"

They all glanced at each other, but the uniform response was a dismissive headshake and shrug. The vehicle was a big four-door white pickup sporting the seal for Canyon State on the front doors. Everyone stood frozen in place, waiting to see what was about to happen.

Two classic cowboys climbed from the pickup and shot smiles at the group before ambling across the yard. By the time they had moved close enough for him to see details of the pair, Seth put them into the category of people he'd like to get to know better.

Canyon State had a reputation of being a program that brought out the best in their rodeo team. They had never been on Zane's list of potential schools, but only because they didn't have the full-ride scholarship. Right now, the smiling men in front of Seth were the best thing he had seen in two weeks. They gave him a hope that had been absent before. When they began to talk, they had everyone's absolute focus.

"Morning, folks. I'm Kirk Jackson and my partner in crime who grins all the time is Bob Gosz. We're faculty in the Range Science Department at Canyon."

They spent several minutes shaking hands then the Canyon State people started explaining again, directing their attention to Zane.

"You probably aren't aware of this, but we have been keeping an eye on your progress over the last two seasons. It has impressed us."

Zane found his voice at a pause in the conversation. "You've been watching me since I was a junior?"

Bob quieted his fellow faculty member. "Kirk didn't quite get the idea across. His explanation sounded a lot more stalkerish and less competitive than we might have wished. So, let me be more direct. We've watched you compete, and you have impressed us. We would like to invite you to join the CSU team. We think it would be to everyone's benefit."

Seth was immediately excited about the possibilities, but Bob had more to say. "We aren't as high profile as some other schools in the state, but what degree are you interested in earning? Our department specializes in animal agriculture. Kirk teaches classes in beef cattle management, ag ecology and ranch diversity."

He turned to Travis. "We've heard about your plans for a rodeo school, as well, and we understand you're interested in a farm-to-table system as part of your whole farm diversification. Our food science faculty members are excited about the opportunity to work with you."

This time Kirk resumed the conversation with his focus on Zane. "A degree from Canyon would prepare you for a variety of positions in agriculture."

"What if I want to major in something outside your department?" Zane said.

Kirk continued with no hesitation. "You can pick from any of our majors. Being on the rodeo team doesn't limit your choices."

Through this conversation Seth moved beside Zane. He had questions of his own. When there was a pause, Seth stepped in with a dad question. "You said there was a scholarship. Could you give us more details?"

Bob chuckled and nodded. "We forget in our excitement sometimes that not everyone knows the program as well as we do. Well, we have all the gory details in the truck, but the quick and dirty facts are that we will cover half of your expenses from your first three-hundred dollar Introduction to Biology textbook to housing in the student apartments" — he winked at Zane — "if you want."

Zane considered a moment. "So, you're offering me the funding for half the expenses for any major."

Kirk nodded. "That's it. Half of the tuition and other costs for riding bulls for our university team."

Zane met Seth's gaze, but neither of them knew what to say. To their good fortune, Travis and Hank had saved them from themselves.

"Hank and TJ are our corporate sponsors. They came out today so they could see how the facility construction was going. Would you guys like to take the tour? I like the idea of working with your faculty on the farm-to-table idea and would love to hear more about that," Travis said. A few minutes later Travis led the group in the general direction of the arena, leaving Zane and Seth alone.

Seth turned to see the shock on his son's face. Then they fell into each other's arms, Seth on the verge of tears. After a rapid recovery, he voiced what was becoming an inevitable verdict.

"There's no reason to not accept the scholarship from Hank. That's an easy decision. You can use it anywhere, and all you have to do is to be a front man for the rodeo and his company."

"And I like root beer," Zane said with a smile.

Seth laughed and nodded. "So, what about the offer from Canyon?"

Zane started ticking off its positive points. "It's a solid state school with tons of majors, and it's a decent distance from home." He locked his eyes on his dad. "They're paying for the other half of my degree. I'd be debt free."

They danced in a circle like two excited kids.

A little bit later, Seth smiled at the group that had gathered around the outdoor kitchen after Travis had completed their tour around the ranch. "Everyone grab a glass of root beer. We need to toast the newest member of Canyon State University's rodeo team."

* * * *

Seth was going through the materials he needed to roll out later that morning. He was wrapping up the presentation he and Travis had been fleshing out. Between Seth, Travis and some people from his old firm, things for the root beer account were progressing pretty well. The one shocking surprise, even to him, was that he'd hired Dave.

He wasn't sure why. It might have been a moment of weakness but his gut told him it had been the right move. Dave still had a tendency to curse like a long-haul trucker but, to his credit, he'd pulled his stuff together since losing Hank's account and was now very familiar with the clients and their product.

It was one thing that Hank had questioned him about right away. He remembered Dave—and not in a good light. But when Seth gave him the option to work with Dave or Seth would find someone else and explained his logic in the hiring, Hank made his decision without hesitation. Seth was flattered that Hank trusted him to that level.

So now they were ready to have their first real client meeting since Hank had rehired Seth. He wasn't certain who was coming. It might be only Hank and George, his dad. Perhaps TJ would be part of the crew this time, which was fine with Seth. He liked Hank's husband, although he couldn't imagine TJ sitting through all the tedious details again. He'd done it once before, though, so Seth would wait and see how things shook out.

Seth studied the campaign. He reminded himself that he was in charge. If Dave acted an ass, he would be out of the door and down the county road before he knew what happened. He'd been warned that it was a certainty if he wasn't on his best behavior.

"This guy doesn't like me. You know that, right?" said Dave.

"He doesn't like you because you acted like an idiot before. You decided their account was not important enough when we were back with Craig's firm." Seth locked his gaze with Dave. "The client is giving you another chance, thanks to me. We've already had this discussion, so there won't be any problems ever again. Right?"

Dave nodded and thumbed through the materials on the table. Seth was including proposals from a variety of angles. The team had agreed that it would be the more effective way of showing the directions they could take the campaign. Seth had met with Hank and TJ several weeks before and gone over the expanded branding they had on the new product lines. They'd liked some of Dave's ideas and Seth had given him credit where credit was due.

"How in the world did you get them to agree to come out here?" Dave said.

"It wasn't my idea. They were the ones who wanted to get out of Fort Worth and into the countryside. They are a sponsor for the rodeo school that Travis has been developing, so it only makes sense that they would want to see the facilities we've been working on. Hopefully, we'll get them out here a lot more often than they have been in the past. We want them to feel their input is valuable, more than a handful of quick visits a year."

Dave fingered the edge of one of the full-color brochures, lost in thought for a few seconds before he started to talk again. "So, who's coming from the company's main office?"

Dave met Seth's gaze, trying to appear innocent and nonchalant. But he still seemed to have some questions about two of the owners being married to each other. That would be one thing he would watch about Dave's attitude.

"I don't know who's coming today, other than Hank. It could be George, could be TJ or all three of them might show up. Why?" Seth lifted an eyebrow.

Dave did a quick dance to avoid taking the questioning any further that direction. "Sounds good. Sounds great. The more the merrier."

Seth was considering making another comment when he heard a vehicle pull into their driveway. He eased the curtain open a crack and saw them park in front of the house. Seth had to chuckle. Hank had decided that his personal branding no longer matched with the silver Lexus he'd driven before. Now he had a four-door Toyota Tundra pickup.

Seth would not comment about it any further, but the truck was every country boy's wet dream. Regardless, he couldn't imagine TJ being anything but urban and stylish. They watched as two familiar figures got out of the pickup.

"Looks like the presentation will be to Hank and TJ. I'm not sure if that makes it easier or harder," Seth said.

Dave took a deep breath then blurted out, "Okay, I'm ready for this. We can do it."

"Damn right we can. This is our only client. If they say we're crawling around the floor after dust mites, then we're hunting for dust mites — whatever it takes to make these people happy. You got that?" Seth said.

"Sure, boss. I know my nuts are hanging by a thread. I plan on pitching this proposal like nothing I've ever pitched before."

"It's not going to be that difficult. They aren't hard-sell clients like we've dealt with before. These people want the look and feel of an old-time soda fountain. We're the ones who convinced them vintage was the way to go. The trick here will be threading our way through the 1950s with contemporary sensibilities."

"Like organic root beer?" Dave said with a smirk.

He studied Dave. "I don't know. They might have organic. I think that would be a pitch you could make to them today."

Dave deflated but kept any further comments to himself as the two of them moved to the front door. Seth opened it just as the pair stepped onto the porch. It surprised Seth that they exchanged hugs and embraces with both him and Dave. Although TJ gave Dave a look that left no doubt in Seth's mind that he knew who Dave was from Hank's previous dealings with the firm.

"Come in, come in. We set up in the dining room. That way we can spread out. Travis hooked up computers, so we have access to anything we need. We're ready to show you our best," Seth said.

They all migrated to chairs around the table. Once everyone had settled into place, Seth launched into the presentation he and Dave had been working on for the last two weeks.

He covered how they would incorporate the new product lines George and Hank had developed with some of their traditional drinks, like the root beer. Seth had also been right about Hank's determination in promoting their product. When they asked about samples, TJ unloaded even more types of beverages than Seth had seen before. They spent the next couple of hours in a more relaxed atmosphere as they tasted the new flavors and discussed how they would tie them into the lines they had already identified.

Seth chuckled to himself when Dave proposed an organic root beer, which the company had sold for twenty years. As the day wore on, Seth started to bring out food samples various caterers had provided. He worked to keep everyone fed so they could stay focused. But despite Seth's best effort, by the middle of the afternoon, the group was losing concentration.

Travis appeared from the patio in his stocking feet, having left his well-worn work boots outside. For the instant it took for his eyes to adjust to the dim interior of the house, Travis froze in place, clearly trying to identify the occupants of the room. It was TJ who saved the moment.

"Travis! My man! How's it hanging today?" TJ said.

Travis broke into a huge grin. Ever since they had become corporate sponsors, Hank and TJ had become two of his favorite people. "TJ! Good, man, really good. Had a few newborn calves this morning, but they're doing fine. The rodeo facilities are coming around with a few potential teachers. It's all starting to come together. Our first class should be mind-blowing." Travis paused for an instant, then plunged onward like a snapping-turtle off a log. "At least this first group is a lock. We've turned away several kids who were wannabe students."

Seth watched all of it with a relaxed ease. His Travis was a natural.

TJ nodded as he walked across the room to exchange handshakes with Travis. Travis handed Hank and TJ fresh drinks. Seth appreciated he had been alert enough to choose bottles they had put in earlier to chill. He stepped back in, took a drink then went to TJ.

"You're serving us ice-cold Hill Country Root Beer," TJ said.

"Absolutely," Travis said as he set his bottle on the glass tabletop, which formed a pool of condensation around the bottle's bottom. With no comment, Travis ducked into the kitchen and came back with a round of appetizers.

"So, how is it going?" Travis asked.

"We settled the details, proofed the final copies and emailed everything to the printer," Seth told him.

Everyone nodded in agreement this time.

Seth continued, "We still have some focus groups to run for the traditional cremes, and you've gotta find some of the more cutting-edge places that would be interested in carrying the newer drinks you've developed. But yeah… Overall, we're ready to roll out the first campaigns."

Travis grinned at TJ. "What do you think? You're more familiar dealing with sharks in the water than I am.

"I think the sharks are tame," TJ said with a laugh.

"Sounds good, really good. So…if y'all are finished with the boring paperwork, we could check out the arena after we finish our refreshments," Travis suggested.

Seth relaxed against the chair and filled his mouth with an enormous swallow of one of the drinks scattered across the table. A few seconds later, Seth realized he wasn't certain what the refreshment he'd chosen was, but he liked it. It was different. Snagging a full bottle, Seth took a long slurp. He studied Hank. "This is great. What is it?"

Hank laughed. "That's one of the alcoholic drinks we've been working on. You'll be feeling damn good for the next few hours."

* * * *

It was the start of the rodeo school they had been working on for six months. For the initial classes, they'd decided they would take only ten kids. Travis hoped it would grow into a lot more than that, but this would kick off the beginning of their plan.

It was fine. The kids were from a mix of backgrounds. Some came from parents who had money and worked in high-rises downtown. But he and Seth had also tried to make it possible for other kids to come to the school as well.

He looked on as another enormous land-barge parked in the driveway. It seemed to be the transportation of choice for these youngsters. Zane was welcoming them and pointing the kids toward the newly finished bunkhouse that had been built to make them feel like they were living on an authentic ranch. The long-term plans were to add more bunkhouses, one for each event.

Travis was a little worried about how they would react. It probably terrified some of them to leave their parents, but he didn't know what kind of indicator, if at all, that would be of their success.

"Some of them are a little skittish, but once they tie into the taco bar Dad set up, they will settle down. Good tacos make everything better," Zane said as he and Amy walked over to where Travis was watching the progress.

He smiled as Zane and Amy flanked him, but he acknowledged Zane's assessment. "Most of them will adjust without any problem. They'll calm down once they make friends. Heck, learning you and Amy won't bite will be a huge difference. They'll feel better when they figure out who they can depend on."

"Yeah, the whole trust thing... It makes life a lot easier," Amy added.

Travis watched Troy lead the last of the students into the bunkhouse. He was the closest to the students' ages and had some experience in riding the small bulls, which gave him even more credibility.

It seemed like everyone who'd paid their entry fees had arrived. Most of them appeared determined, which was all Travis could hope for.

Seth joined them to watch students being toured through the ranch by Troy, and their parents entertained for a few minutes by James.

They had agreed several weeks before that the faster they got the parents and the kids separated, the better it would be for everybody. The last thing that any of the youngsters needed was a hysterical mother or father who didn't know how to let go of their kid. Travis understood that they were trying to do what was best for the children but he also knew that was hard sometimes.

"We need to wrap it up. I think the parents should be heading out. Let's hook up for that first hayride to start the activities after the tacos. Then tomorrow, we learn how to be rodeo cowboys," Travis said.

The group broke into their assigned duties. All of them were concerned at how this would go, but they had been discussing it for weeks and it was time to earn their wages.

The parents all left without drama, the tacos and the hayride went great and the first night was uneventful, not a homesick student in the bunch. Seth got everyone going bright and early with a full breakfast, and Travis began the classes in earnest. He was thrilled that the next couple of days went very well too.

Several days passed with Zane and Dustin working with the potential bull riders. Not surprisingly, one of them decided it wasn't for him and left for home. But then something happened that sent Travis into shock.

Amy came to him and asked to replace the bull rider who'd left. "You said you'd let girls in. I want to try bull riding. The pole bending and barrel races are too tame for me. I want to show the boys how it's done."

Travis' first response was a resounding 'no way', but then he thought more about it and decided it shouldn't make any difference. Seth hadn't stopped Zane from riding bulls, so he didn't know why he should stop Amy — other than she was his baby and he wanted to protect her every second that she breathed. But that was the reaction from every parent.

The first couple of times she rode, his heart was in his throat and his stomach knotted. But it became evident that she could handle herself just fine, down to the two-point landing off her first bull. Travis relaxed at little, at least when she was climbing onto the animal. He always was where he should be. With Shane being the bullfighter for the kids, she was in the best hands possible. But Superman and Thor could have been the bullfighters for Amy and he still would have worried some.

"Makes you want to puke a little bit, doesn't it?" Seth said.

Seth leaned over and wrapped his arm around his cowboy's shoulder.

Travis nodded. "You know you're right, otherwise you wouldn't be so smug about it. And I don't see how you made it through all those times with Zane. I think I would've been on anti-anxiety medication."

Seth chuckled but Travis could tell he was sympathizing with him. "It was all I could do not to jump into the arena, grab Zane and drag him to safety. But I managed."

Seth motioned to the activity in the arena. "Amy is about to have her round. We need to watch."

A second later the dark-haired girl looked like a tick on the top of the huge bull she was riding when it burst out of the chute and bucked a trail across the arena.

The two of them worked together in an unwilling partnership. But the way things were progressing, she was doing an excellent job. Travis had made it through the timed event without jumping over the fence to save his baby, even though he was close by the time the eight seconds had elapsed. A second or two later, she bailed off the bull. She landed with her hat in one hand, waving to the crowd, even though the loudest part of the throng was her father and Seth.

"See? I told you she was good. Another year practicing with Zane and she will go for the scholarship."

Travis' mouth gaped open, the possibility making him queasy. His little girl turning into a bull rider... He wasn't sure what to think. But, as Seth had pointed out, he had time. At least two seasons of travel and all of them to help her. Then he realized Seth had ended the conversation and refocused.

"Zane can help her too. It's not like he will spend his entire life studying and practicing. When he travels with the college team, she might even ride with them," Seth suggested.

But as Travis considered that last thought, he decided his sixteen-year-old daughter was not going to be alone with a bunch of horny college teenagers, so that was something he'd have to work out. Issues like that had been part of the reason he'd kept his daughter away from bull riders, and now she was gonna be one of them.

His hand started its nervous twitch and he fought to hide his reaction. He and Seth reevaluated the bullfighters and Travis was shocked at who stood beside Shane.

"Dammit, it's Troy."

Before they could launch into some kind of overblown rescue mission, James materialized. "That's something, isn't it? I about crapped myself when the boy came to me and told me he'd changed his mind and that he doesn't want to be a bull rider anymore. He wants to be a bullfighter. Talk about going from the skillet to the fire. But I had several long, agonizing talks with Shane. He knows me. If I'm determined, then I do it. Troy's not any different. At least Shane is around with some expert advice. He's not getting half-ass information from the people who only think they know what they're talking about."

"I can see how little boys setting goals makes all of us better teachers. It seems like a good idea to me," Seth said.

James shrugged again. "Shane is talented. He has great natural reactions."

The three of them stood watching the spectacle play out as Shane and Troy coaxed the bull back into the pen and the crowd realized the bull riding competition had ended.

Zane glanced across the small group then said, "Don't try to make him into something you want. Let him write his own set of rules, with your input. If he wants to be a cowboy, then for God's sake let him do it. The same thing with Amy. If she wants to ride bulls, you will *not* change her mind. I don't know why you would even think you can." Zane stayed quiet as the others glanced at him with various levels of fear and admiration on their faces.

"When did you become the adult?" Seth said.

Zane smiled then arched his eyebrows up and down, imitating Groucho Marx. It told Travis that they had done everything they'd needed to for their kids.

* * * *

As the week progressed, things went better than they'd hoped. Only the one student had left early, and they thought he might come back in a later session.

Hank and TJ joined Travis at the grandstand. They had funded a decent sound system, another tidbit that made it possible for the rodeo school to appear more professional. Travis shook hands with each of the two men he was coming to think of as close friends.

"Are you guys enjoying the festivities?"

TJ gazed toward Hank for a moment then turned to Travis. "This is one of the smartest things we've done... That's how both of us feel about this. You can't imagine how many of these parents grew up on George's formulation for root beer. It's taking them back to a time when their lives were simpler and seemed better." He chuckled. "They weren't really any better, but we're selling the nostalgia. So, we have no intentions of telling them anything otherwise. The millennials with kids—God help us all—love the mix of food trucks out of Dallas-Fort Worth. I have to admit that I don't mind you have something besides white-bread buns with wieners and yellow mustard. But then, I'm partial to the Korean tacos. Delicious."

Seth gave Travis a grin as he walked up to join the crowd. He motioned toward Dustin and Shane, who were talking with some parents. "They'll be here soon. They're answering questions from fans."

"The bull fighting is a big crowd-pleaser, but it makes me nervous. Just the idea of any fourteen-year-old kid teasing a fifteen-hundred-pound animal in the arena leaves me with a bad set of hives," Seth said. "I know that for sure."

Travis couldn't contain a laugh. "Hives?"

"Okay, maybe hives wasn't the best medical choice. But it does make me break out in something nasty."

The rodeo school ran to its conclusion on Saturday afternoon. By the time he had talked to the last set of parents, Travis was sure all the kids had learned a lot during the week he'd had them but he was exhausted.

He wanted to assure himself that everyone had enjoyed a good time. Even if they didn't keep riding bulls, he wanted them to have gained a lifetime of memories. More importantly, he'd worked with Hank to have the best promotion Hill Country Root Beer had ever pulled off. They'd also invited a few of the premier food trucks from the metroplex and the chefs had run with all their suggestions.

"They're all gone — every blessed one of them," Seth said.

"Good. I appreciate them all. Everyone left with a grin on their face." The people involved with his school had covered their responsibilities in impressive ways. "But it's time for everyone to go back home and for us to have the ranch to ourselves for a few weeks."

Chapter Eleven

Travis watched the scene below him unfold as he always did – like someone testing the shower spray to see if it was going to be too hot, too cold or just right. The day had started with something rare for northern Texas, layers of dense fog wrapped around their headquarters. He let the mare's reins slip over her mane and looped his leg around the saddle horn. The sense of peace became even more comforting as the tendrils of fog slipped closer. Travis caught the brim of his hat with his index finger and cocked it back. A few seconds earlier he had heard the soft scrape of hoof against limestone. *Someone's coming.*

Travis twisted and flashed a greeting as Seth came through the curtain of fog which had thickened. "Morning, Seth."

Seth guided his horse beside Travis' mount. They sat there for several minutes, enjoying each other's company.

Seth couldn't keep from chuckling. "Out surveying your kingdom, sire?"

Travis swatted his hand playfully at Seth. "Damn straight I am. But could you have imagined all this a year ago? The house, the rough arena the kids had been using—and that was it. Now, everything is new and improved. There's a professional kitchen for the foodies and we have the rodeo school and a new house for James and Troy. At this point, who knows what else we might come up with."

Seth visibly tensed when the mare he was on shifted her weight, causing him to hesitate. By the time she had swished her tail a few times, Seth had settled into a more comfortable position. Travis smiled. "Zane told me your riding abilities have improved. Now you're good enough to ride into the arena, make a few announcements and get back out without falling off."

Seth snorted. "Yes, he told me if we're going to set up the headquarters to serve as a dude ranch, then I have to act the part of the land baron—and that includes being able to ride a horse to the point where I don't bounce off when it hits a gait faster than a walk."

"You know what the most surprising success has been for me?" Travis asked.

"It's too long a list to pick from. What would be your favorite?"

"The day I walked into the bank, closed all of our accounts and told Frank he and his board were a poor judge of who's a bad risk for credit."

Travis savored a smile between the two of them as Seth squeezed the inside of his thigh. An errant beam of morning light broke through the haze and brought him back to the current flurry of activities taking place below them. It was amazing how routine it had all become over the past year and the amount it had grown.

They had become a premier tourist destination for those wanting to experience life on a real working ranch, and they had a horde of dedicated foodies on a waiting list for their monthly farm-to-table presentations, which gave them a level of financial security. The popularity of those occasions had reached a notoriety that neither of them had expected. On top of the more obvious benefits to Travis' homestead, a whole local industry was developing around providing for those events.

Travis and Seth had met with chefs from the metroplex who were competing for the chance to create a meal, and they had re-energized the economy of the area surrounding the ranch for everything from free-range eggs to fresh vegetables in season. "It's amazing that we found this many people to work with. I wouldn't have thought we could have located the range of food resources we've managed," Travis mused.

"You're quite the recruiter, Seth. If they had left it to me, we would be lucky if we had grilled hamburgers once a year. But you seemed to find somebody that fits well with each farmers market we searched."

Seth grinned at his lover and listen to the early morning sounds coming from the ranch. "It's been busy, though there was a complication here and there. But not only has the food thing taken off more than we could ever imagine, but the rodeo school is a winner on several levels too."

Travis let out a chuckle. "Yes, two more bunkhouses and we will cover every event. We may need to build a second arena too — one for the timed events. But so far, we've not had problems filling a quarterly school calendar. We also have a list of people wanting to teach, including Dustin and Shane.

"They're excited all right," said Seth. "We're getting a reputation for the ranch. And besides, they're only offering bull riding and bullfighting in their school. But we're working on more advanced levels, so it's easy to tie to them as a second-tier school for any of their students who want to advance. Zane and Amy are gathering kudos for their skills too. Besides his university winning at the national competition, Zane made the Dean's Honor Role both semesters. The coaches for the team keep them on a short leash, so there have been none of the freshmen stunts to avoid. There is even talk of him being team captain. I'm thrilled with how things have worked out."

Travis grew a smile that stretched from ear to ear. "Amy is doing well too. Letting her ride bulls cured the issues she had and she's more excited about competition now than she ever was. So, all's good. And, of course, our relationship is amazing."

Seth was about to reply when they heard airbrakes below them and watched as two white refrigerated trucks pulled into the driveway.

Great. Right in the middle of everything.

Travis waited a few seconds then sighed. "Another newbie. I'd better go make sure he doesn't sit there with a bunch of perishable heirloom lettuce that is the keynote of supper." Travis let his horse's reins slide down its neck with practiced ease. But before he could get far, Seth's fingers closed around his arm.

Seth pulled him close and whispered in his ear. "You know the kids want a wedding, right?"

Travis tensed for a minute then sagged against Seth. "Yeah, I know. Amy finds some way every day to remind me she wants to give me away."

"Does that present a problem for you?" Seth asked.

"No. Absolutely not. Nothing is an issue about me being married to you. It's just…"

"Just to let you know… I agree with Zane and Amy on this one. You don't have to do anything but show up. We will be the planners for the wedding, and I'm sure we can find enough people involved in the catering industry to create a fabulous and amazing reception."

"All right. I get the message loud and clear. I want to be legally married too." Travis stood beside him for several long seconds. "Is a June wedding too traditional?"

"Not at all. I always thought I would make a great June bride."

Want to see more like this?
Here's a taster for you to enjoy!

Roughstock: Blind Ride
BA Tortuga

Excerpt

Jason stood there with the big fake check for the event win, watching the crowd go one of two ways — up and out of the stands, or down to wait for the guys to make the autograph circuit. He fucking hated this part.

That little broad from the XSports channel was waiting with her bright orange hair and her too tight jeans. He knew how it'd go, too. *Blah blah blah Jason Scott blah blah blah race for the finals blah blah blah new kids chasing his ass.*

Goodie.

He managed to get through all the questions without being an asshole, but not before a huge stack of fans were hanging over the fence, waving programs and hats, hollering his name. He ducked under into the pens and headed toward the back. He just wasn't good at that whole meet-and-greet thing.

"You're gonna get a reputation as an asshole, man." His best buddy, Andy Baxter, fell in beside him, boots clacking against the concrete walkway back to the locker room.

"Yeah, yeah. Better let them think I might be than know I am. 'sides, I don't see your happy ass out there, Bax."

And shit, nine times out of ten Bax was out there glad-handing.

"It was a long night. My knee's killin' me."

That slow Texas drawl always made him smile, because it made everyone think Bax was laid-back, maybe not so bright.

Jason knew better.

"Yeah?" He winced, shook his head. "You came down on it fucking hard. I swear that bull has it out for you."

It was hell getting old.

"I did." Bax shrugged, sticking his hands in the pockets of his old school Wranglers. "I ain't the man of steel I used to be."

"Bullshit." There wasn't any bastard on Earth tough as Bax. He knew it to the bone. "You want to go get a steak?"

"Hell, yes. Someplace not at the hotel." They were staying at the sanctioned hotel because the sponsors had asked Jason to, but eating there was like sitting in a fishbowl.

"I got the truck here. We can go anywhere." He nodded to Little Jack and Harvey who were still waiting outside sports medicine. DJ had taken one hell of a spill, just got caught up and dragged. "Y'all heard something?"

Jack shook his head. "They ain't called the am'blance. That's gotta be good, huh?"

"I guess."

"Well, you call me, you hear something, yeah?" Bax said, nodding. "Come on, man. Food."

"I hear you, old man." He winked at Jack, headed off, following that tight little ass to get their gear.

"Not that much older than you, Mini." Bax took every opportunity to give him shit about how much shorter he was.

"Three years is a fucking eternity." He ducked the lazy swing, just hooting with it. "You still scattered from the round, man? You missed."

"You were on the move. Stand up and let me hit you, man." That laugh was sure enough the best way to make him forget all the shit his sponsors wished he would do.

"Fuck you." He started stripping off his shirt, hunting something clean and less dusty.

"Here." One of his hanging shirts landed on his shoulder. "That one looks good on."

"Thanks." He redid the smell-good, the deodorant. Then he changed his boots. "Man, I need a beer."

"We can have that with supper. Or, hey, we could go play some pool." Oh, yeah, because Bax wanted to shark that five thousand he'd won in the second go-round.

"We could do both. Hell, after a steak, I might feel ten years younger." He got himself put together, tucked in his shirt and got his belt buckled. Okay. Wallet. Phone. Bag. Time to get out of Dodge. "Besides, all the buckle bunnies'll be gone home by late."

"True enough." They went out the back way, Bax's white shirt setting off his deep tan, that black hat playing hide and seek with Bax's dark brown eyes and smile lines.

Jason tossed his gear into the back, thumping his cock but good as it did its dead-level best to wake up and say hello and howdy to Bax.

Good night. You'd think he was a Brazilian after a good ride. *Down boy.*

Bax threw his duffel back, too, sliding into the driver's side. "So, where to? I figure that one little place where you circle your order will be closed."

"There's that one place by the highway—about twenty minutes out. It's nothing but old ranchers taking their women out. Nice T-bones." And he always got tickled by those tables with the ads printed on them. Reminded him of going to auction with Pa-paw.

"That works." The big dualie slid into traffic like an elephant into a herd of zebras, Bax muscling them right in.

They scooted down 35, radio blaring. He found a pack of smokes in the console and lit one for Bax, then got himself one. Three days of rest, then Tulsa.

"You think we ought to try and hit home 'fore Tulsa?"

It was kinda eerie sometimes, the way Bax read his mind. Then again, they'd been on the road together for nigh on six years.

"We can. Momma'd like to see us. 'Course, we could go on to the city. Goof off. Depends on how much you want Momma's pineapple upside down cake."

"Oh, I'd rather go see your momma." That man did have a sweet tooth. Pineapple upside down was Bax's very favorite.

"Cool. I'll call her. Let her know we'll be in." He took a deep drag, grinned. *Lord, lord.* "I hope your knee's up to riding fence."

"Shit, you know it. Just don't ask me to walk fence." Wheeling around a little Honda, Bax started humming with George on the radio, off tune as anything.

"Nah. You wouldn't be worth shit in Tulsa, then."

They both hooted, and Jason leaned back, easy in his bones.

Man, event win number three. Check in his pocket. Him and Bax heading for steak.

Life, she was good.

PUBLISHING

Sign up for our newsletter and find out about all our romance book releases, eBook sales and promotions, sneak peeks and FREE romance books!

About the Author

Jon Keys' earliest memories revolve around books; with the first ones he can recall reading himself being "The Warlord of Mars" and anything with Tarzan. (The local library wasn't particularly up to date.) But as puberty set in, he started sneaking his mother's romance magazines and added the world of romance and erotica to his mix of science fiction, fantasy, Native American, westerns and comic books.

A voracious reader for almost half a century, Jon has only recently begun creating his own flights of fiction for the entertainment of others. Born in the Southwest and now living in the Midwest, Jon has worked as a ranch hand, teacher, computer tech, roughneck, designer, retail clerk, welder, artist, and, yes, pool boy; with interests ranging from kayaking and hunting to painting and cooking, he draws from a wide range of life experiences to create written works that draw the reader in and wrap them in a good story.

Jon loves to hear from readers. You can find his contact information, website details and author profile page at https://www.pride-publishing.com